Humans, Practicing
by Megan Carney

Copyright © 2021 by Megan Carney

All rights reserved. No part of this publication may be reproduced, distributed, or transmitted in any form or by any means, including photocopying, recording, or other electronic or mechanical methods, without the prior written permission of the publisher, except in the case of brief quotations embodied in critical reviews and certain other noncommercial uses permitted by copyright law.

The characters, names, and events as well as all places, incidents, organizations, and dialog in this novel are either the products of the writer's imagination or are used fictitiously.

Cover art by JohnBellArt.

Previous titles by Megan Carney

Sarina, Sweetheart
Trap and Trace (A Navy Trent book)
From Hackerville with Love (A Navy Trent book)

Learn more about Megan Carney at megancarney.com.

ISBN-13: 978-1734759020

To all the broken, beautiful people in the world trying to find their way home.

Chapter 1 4

Chapter 2 7

Chapter 3 14

Chapter 4 18

Chapter 5 35

Chapter 6 42

Chapter 7 54

Chapter 8 66

Chapter 9 71

Chapter 10 84

Chapter 11 91

Chapter 12 94

Chapter 13 100

Chapter 14 114

Chapter 15 118

Chapter 16 127

Chapter 17 133

Chapter 18 136

Chapter 19 140

Chapter 20 148

Chapter 21 153

Chapter 22 158

Chapter 25 161

Chapter 26 163

Chapter 27 169

Chapter 28 175

Chapter 29 188

Chapter 30 191

Chapter 31 197

Chapter 32 208

Epilogue 220

Acknowledgments 229

Chapter 1

Navy Trent could have gone a lifetime without seeing this photo again. The photo had been taken the morning after she killed her would-be assassin, when she was leaving the hotel room with the secret service agents the U.S. government had provided for her protection. She had felt bruised and tired and overwhelmed. And for weeks afterward, this image of her face had circulated on the news and in the papers everywhere.

"I feel you," Navy muttered to the image of herself.

She had been working on this puzzle for hours. The close-up of her face didn't exactly match the old news article; the image was pixelated in odd places. And there was a scattering of red dots in the lower left-hand corner that stood out. The picture was altered. And whoever had altered it wanted her to know it was altered.

Someone had broken into the CIA's payroll server and left this one file. They could have taken the names and addresses of every employee, but instead they had left this. Her face.

The picture was a message. Someone had hidden data inside the file. Using a picture of her was just the attacker's way of addressing the envelope. A message that she hadn't yet managed to decrypt.

Strong hands landed on her shoulders. She jumped, even though the touch was familiar. "I said I'd be there soon," Navy said without looking away from the screen.

Jackson's deep laugh was right next to her. His freshly shaved skin rubbed against her earlobe. "I told you the pizza was here an hour ago. You're doing that thing again."

She pretended innocence. "What thing?"

"That thing where you get so wrapped up in work you forget it's Saturday, and I'm only home in DC for two weeks." He kissed her neck. "And would very much like your attention."

"But I just need—"

Jackson held his watch in front of her. It was a tactical watch. Capable of withstanding freezing temperatures, submersion in water up to 100 meters, all the while keeping time in every time zone around the world.

"It's nearly eleven. You've been working on this all night." He massaged her shoulders, digging his thumbs into the tightness near her spine. "Take a break. Let your subconscious work on the problem for a while."

She rolled her shoulders as the muscles relaxed. "Your fancy psychological secret agent tricks won't work on me."

"Then it won't hurt to kiss me," he said with infuriating confidence.

"This is a message." She stabbed the screen with her finger. "A message about me, or for me, or... threatening me. I've used every steganography program I know to pull out the message. And it's just garbage. It's encrypted. I have to find the key."

He cleared his throat. "I may just be Jackson Fletcher, lowly CIA field agent and technological idiot, but if someone wanted to send a message to you, and they wanted to be sure only you could read it, wouldn't they use that PGP key thing you were trying to explain to me the other day?"

Her mouth dropped open. "Of course." A few simple commands later, the decrypted message appeared on her screen. She turned to glare at him. "Don't you dare tell anyone at work."

"Your reputation as a CIA geek is safe with me."

"Cybersecurity analyst," she corrected.

"CIA g—" He stopped as he read the words on the screen. "Navy, you should look at this."

She rubbed at her tired eyes to make sure the late hour wasn't causing hallucinations.

```
My name is Kor Min Gyu, or Min Gyu Kor
as you would say in the West. I work in
Office 91. I want to defect. I can destroy
the furniture factory. Email and PGP key
follow this message.
```

"North Korea," Navy said softly. "Office 91 is North Korea's cyber weapons division. But what's the furniture factory?"

"I don't know. That's not my corner of the world. You can ask when you meet with Defections."

Navy groaned. "Meet with? Can't I just pass the message on? We're short-staffed already because of the crappy flu season."

"Sorry." Jackson squeezed her shoulder. "He contacted you for a reason. Defections will want to figure out why."

The image of her face seemed even more sinister next to Min Gyu's cryptic message. The full photo had appeared in one of the many front page stories about Navy above the headline "Patriot or Traitor?" Maybe the would-be defector from North Korea wasn't sure if he was a patriot or a traitor either. She read the words again, wishing she could hear them. Was it a genuine plea for help? Or was he a Trojan horse in human form?

Chapter 2

Min Gyu hated concrete. He hated how it crumbled at the corners on all the buildings he could see. He hated how paint fell away in chunks instead of flakes, leaving Pyongyang gray under almost any light, including the tepid dawn that accompanied this morning's walk to work. And his apartment was on the "good" side of the city.

At the corner, a traffic cop stood crisply in the middle of the intersection, despite the fact the broad street was empty of cars. A white circle marked the borders of her concrete platform. The lighter blue of the umbrella protecting her from the nonexistent sun clashed with her neatly ironed navy-blue skirt. The windows of Pyongyang Department Store No. 1 were so clean they sparkled. Inside, shelves of goods advertised the wealth and normalcy of North Korea's citizens. Except that when the store opened in a couple hours, it was unlikely any customers would come. The only people who shopped there were aid workers, foreign diplomats, and the occasional high-ranking party member. Some of the goods stocked weren't even for sale, they were just there to supply the illusion of abundance.

Less than a mile ahead, Min Gyu could see the gleaming, rocket-like structure of the Ryugyong Hotel. The hotel had been under construction for nearly twenty years. At one point, it could have been the tallest hotel in the world—had they finished the damn thing before someone built a taller one. But they hadn't and now it was just another punch line in the terrible joke that was North Korea.

A hotel with no guests. Streets with no cars. Department stores with products they didn't intend to sell to customers who would never come.

He could have laughed except even here, when he could see no one, he knew he was being watched. Not that it mattered. If he bothered to laugh at everything ridiculous in his country, he would have died laughing a long time ago.

Min Gyu's only solace was these walks. He lit a cigarette and inhaled deeply. He smoked his father's brand, Camel, rather than the more fashionable, patriotic 7.27 Victory cigarettes.

He could have taken the meticulously clean but shabby metro to shorten his commute. He wanted to be alone.

Everyone, everywhere studied each other for signs of impure thoughts. A blink too slow or too fast that might indicate you did not believe that evil, imperialist Americans started the Korean war. A slip of the tongue that could betray your doubt in the brilliance and magnificence of Kim Jong Eun. Even in dark bedrooms, lovers avoided discussing politics.

Too soon he arrived at the squat, two-story concrete building in the Mankyungdae district. Like everything else, it was slowly falling apart. Most people who knew what he did envied him. He was watched because he was trusted with access most North Koreans would never have. From his desk, he could visit the *New York Times* website. Sure, the desks were made sometime in the early nineties, before the Soviet Union fell and stopped writing blank checks to their Communist neighbor, but he was part of the elite. He was a cyber warrior, a defender of Juche thought.

Once, as a perk, his unit had been given a trip to Kaesong. On the train, a farmer with a gaunt face had accosted him.

Min Gyu still remembered the thin, surprisingly strong fingers gripping his arm so hard they left creases on the sleeve of his uniform.

"You must be so honored." The farmer's wide, glistening eyes had focused first on the stripes and bars of Min Gyu's uniform that marked him as part of the cyber corps, then on Min Gyu's face. "You can demonstrate your love for the Dear Leader in your work every day."

At the time, Min Gyu had taken the words at face value. There were plenty of people who never doubted the regime's propaganda. Hardly surprising, given that children were essentially raised in state-run schools. But looking back, Min Gyu saw something different in his memory of the farmer's eyes. Jealousy. Cyber warriors were allocated apartments with heat in cities where electricity was semi-reliable. They were given sufficient rations, enough to eat rice at every meal.

The cost was spending most of his days in this suffocating office, attacking the rest of the world for having the audacity to do better than North Korea at pretty much everything. Only one of his fellow cyber warriors, Young Sun, was there. Young Sun didn't even look up from his keyboard. Min Gyu was grateful. He was here early because there was something he had to do.

He put his lunch pail on his desk and sat down, cursing the too-short sleeves of his stiff uniform jacket. His sergeant, Chul Hwan, insisted that Min Gyu was mistaken about the measurements being wrong. Min Gyu knew better. Cloth shortages meant uniforms in the right size weren't always available.

Min Gyu's nerves were affecting his focus. His task had to be completed while the office was nearly empty, and before his sergeant showed up. His computer was a clunky desktop from sometime in the last three years. A sticker on the outside proclaimed it was the property of an elementary school in Germany. Another castoff smuggled into the country because very few countries would do business with North Korea.

The second his fingers touched the keyboard his shoulders stiffened. Everything he typed or clicked was recorded. He logged in, then checked on the various scans that were still running, to keep up appearances. Min Gyu glanced up to make sure his coworker wasn't watching.

This was the tricky part. Min Gyu couldn't just disable the keylogger; his watchers would notice the interruption. He had to substitute legitimate activity. He hoped his replay code was good enough. It had been so far. When Min Gyu held down *f, k, j,* and *e* at the same time, the cursor on his terminal blinked "OK" in Morse code. It was the signal that he had activated his program, nicknamed "Mirage." His superiors thought Mirage was a piece of malware designed to intercept and modify packets on victim machines. It wasn't a fancy idea, or a new idea, which meant they didn't look at it too closely.

Typically, such malware was deployed to steal money from bank accounts. When the victim logged into their favorite bank, they would see their account balance as they expected. In the background, Mirage initiated a series of transfers that would empty the account. But all the user would ever see was their original balance, because of how Mirage modified the packets before they reached the web browser.

Min Gyu had adapted the malware for a slightly different use. For the next five minutes, Mirage would intercept the packets sent by the keylogger and modify them so his activity mimicked what he had done when he first sat down at his desk. Like replaying a loop of video when hacking a security camera.

He logged into Gmail, using the address he'd given Navy Trent. The circle on his browser spun as the page loaded slowly. Another thing to curse in this ridiculous country. Their office had the best connection in Pyongyang, but it was still unreliable and lethargic. There were only two ways out of the country, one to a telecom in China and when that failed, a satellite. Min Gyu glanced around again, then worried that he was making himself look suspicious. His list of messages was blank. She hadn't made contact. They must have shown her the image. She must have decoded it by now.

He didn't know how much longer he could wait. He closed the browser and deactivated Mirage. She would email him tomorrow, he promised himself. Or the day after that. She knew what it was like to have an entire government set against her. She had defied a president. Surely, she would save him.

"Kor Min Gyu," a deep voice behind him said.

Min Gyu spun his chair around too quickly. He had lost his focus again. He could not afford mistakes. Young Sun was already standing at attention, his right hand in a crisp salute. Min Gyu followed suit. The man who had startled Min Gyu now stood in front of him.

"I am Kim Yung Bo, from State Security," the man said. As if every North Korean didn't already know how to recognize a State Security officer. Min Gyu's apartment was bugged. Everyone who worked here was under audio surveillance. Had Min Gyu said something in his sleep?

"We are honored by your presence." Min Gyu tried to force some feeling into the mechanical phrase. State Security had never visited the office when his sergeant was gone.

Yung Bo's answer was a wolfish smile. The slight paunch at his waistband spoke of power. Even the middle class went without food sometimes. Yung Bo studied each desk in the room. Most had pictures of family on them. Min Gyu's did not. Still smiling, Yung Bo walked to the wall where the pictures of the leaders were displayed.

Every house, apartment, and office in the country was supposed to display three portraits: the Great Leader Kim Il Sung, the Dear Leader Kim Jong Il, and the Supreme Leader Kim Jong Eun. The State Security officer ran a fingertip along the gilded frame, and held up the result for their benefit.

"No dust," Yung Bo said. "That is good. Where are your colleagues and your sergeant? They are late."

No one was late. The statement was a test. Contradicting an officer of such high rank bordered on treason. On the other hand, anything bad he said about his sergeant would lead to punishment later. Yung Bo could send Min Gyu to a prison camp with a snap of his fingers. Min Gyu's sergeant could make his daily life hell.

Min Gyu bowed slightly, taking the opportunity to confirm Yung Bo's rank by counting the stars on his patches. "I am sorry, Commander Kim. I was so focused on exalting the Supreme Leader, I did not think to ask where they went." He was glad the bow hid his face from view. Of course, it also meant Min Gyu couldn't read Yung Bo's reaction.

"What is your project, comrade?" Yung Bo asked.

Min Gyu straightened. Out of the corner of his eye, he saw jealousy in his coworker's expression. "To break into the CIA's payroll server so we can find their bastard agents, Commander." Every dictator needed an enemy to keep the populace in line. In North Korea, the Americans were blamed for everything from rice shortages to the annual flu season.

"A good idea." Yung Bo's nod of approval seemed genuine. "The Party is eager to hear your results."

Shit. He'd told his sergeant what his project was, just so he didn't have to hide his activity targeting the CIA's network. But he'd never wanted attention from the upper ranks. He bowed his head again. "I am sorry I have nothing to report yet."

The officer raised one eyebrow to signal his disappointment.

"I will work all night," Min Gyu said. He kept his face blank to avoid sneering on his next words. "I will work all night for the glory of our Great Leader." Min Gyu would not work all night. His sergeant would send him home. Extra hours of work meant extra hours his sergeant had to review the logs of his activity.

The wolfish smile was back on Yung Bo's face. Like he was still on the hunt. "Our leaders have sacrificed so much for us, it is only right that we make sacrifices for them."

Sacrificed, Min Gyu thought bitterly as Yung Bo left. There were over a hundred villas scattered around the country just for the Supreme Leader. In the nineties, when gangs of starving children orphaned by hunger wandered the countryside, Kim Il Sung died fat in his bed.

Chapter 3

Jackson's phone rattled on the nightstand. He groaned inwardly, then pulled his arm from around Navy and rolled over. His work was dangerous and kept him away from home for extended periods of time. But when he was home, work generally left him alone.

Navy stirred, rubbed her eyes, and looked at the clock. "Six a.m. On a Sunday. Seriously?"

"Go back to sleep," Jackson said. "It's just Kevin." He realized his mistake before he finished the last syllable. Kevin was his handler. He didn't make social calls.

"Kevin never calls this early on your weeks off."

"I'm sure it's nothing." Jackson pulled one knee up and leaned a forearm on it before answering. "This better be good."

"What in God's name did you step in?" Kevin's voice sounded like he had just woken up too.

"You're the one who woke me up. What's going on?"

"Defections wants to meet with Navy, about that message she got. You should go with her."

"Of course they'll want to meet with her. I already told her that."

Kevin made a sound between a sigh and a huff. It was the sound he made when Jackson wasn't getting it. "Defections wants to meet with her *today*. And you should go with her."

To a defector, calling the hotline or sending an email was a life-changing moment. To Defections, it was just one of hundreds of messages they received daily. And since organizing a defection required multiple departments and agencies, there was no point in calling Navy in on a Sunday. Everyone would be in the office tomorrow. "All she has to do is pass the message on and explain she doesn't know the guy who sent it. What are you not telling me?"

"The furniture factory." Kevin enunciated the words carefully. "You don't know what that means, do you?"

"I can translate it into Pashto for you."

"The first nuclear research facility in North Korea was called the Yongbyon Furniture Factory. The defector is saying he can destroy North Korea's nuclear weapons program if we get him out."

Jackson whistled softly. "I see why you're worried." If the defector was telling the truth, an operation like this would make or break several careers. Having Navy in the mix, given her past, posed a risk for her.

"She doesn't know this guy right, right?"

Navy grabbed the phone and hit the speaker button. "If you're going to talk about me, at least let me listen."

"Good morning to you, too," Kevin said. "This guy that contacted you, you don't know him, right?"

Her brow wrinkled with confusion. "Of course not. How would I know anyone from North Korea?"

"Are you sure?" Kevin asked. "This is important."

"You're being more annoying than usual. Can we skip ahead to the part where you tell me what's going on?"

"Furniture factory is code for North Korea's nuclear weapons program," Kevin said. Jackson knew Kevin well enough to imagine his expression, brows angled down, eyes narrowed. "This is big. We have to follow up on this lead. They're going to dissect your history to find out why he chose you. And if the operation doesn't go well, or someone thinks the defection is a fake, the blame will have to go somewhere. So think very carefully. Is there any reason, anything in your past, that might connect you to this guy?"

Navy leaned her head against Jackson's shoulder and laced her arm through his. "I don't know anyone who even lives in that hemisphere. I swear."

"Good," Kevin said. "When you meet with Defections, be polite and helpful, but don't get involved. Disengage as soon as you can."

She closed her eyes and let out a slow breath. "Got it. Disengage."

"I'll be there if I can make it," Kevin said.

"If you can make it?" Jackson asked.

"Kevin?" a woman's voice asked in the background, barely discernible, as if from another room.

Jackson exchanged an amused look with Navy. "Where exactly are you?"

"A friend's house," Kevin said.

"A friend you met last night at a bar?"

"I'm outside DC, so it's a bit of a drive." Kevin's voice changed to a casual tone, for the benefit of whomever had walked into the room. "If traffic's good, I'll make it."

"If you want a ride to your car, we have to leave now," the woman said in the background, much closer now. "I have work."

"Sounds like a real love connection," Jackson said.

Kevin hung up on him.

The headboard creaked as both Navy and Jackson leaned against it. "Do you think the plea is real?" Navy asked. "Or just a trick?"

He kissed the part in her hair. "Let Defections worry about that. Just tell them what you know and disengage, like Kevin said."

Her head shook against his shoulder. "I thought I had earned everyone's trust. No one's said anything bad about my work. I even did that undercover thing last year with

16

the Romanian crime ring. I thought all the accusations of being a traitor were behind me."

"It's complicated." Jackson studied the ceiling, wondering if he should sugarcoat things. No, she'd never liked that. "Half the CIA thinks you did the right thing telling the world about CRYSTAL. There are a lot of people who spent years working internal channels trying to shut that project down. Half of them don't trust their own mothers. Hell, I know people who are still bitter that Ellsberg released the *Pentagon Papers*."

She traced circles on his thin cotton T-shirt. "So I'll always be working under a cloud."

"Do you regret coming to work for the company?" Jackson didn't know if he wanted to hear the answer. Her work at the CIA made his life easier. It meant she had a reason to live in DC, where he was based. It meant that his relationship with her was under less scrutiny.

"No, I'd get more attention elsewhere. Last time I visited my parents the local paper took pictures of us while we were eating dinner."

"The hometown hero?"

"Depends on who you ask. It's like you said, I guess. I've had people come up and tell me how brave I was. I've had homeless veterans spit on me."

This time it was her phone rattling on the nightstand.

"That'll be Defections calling to set up the meeting," he said. "Remember—"

"Be polite, be helpful, and disengage. I got it."

Chapter 4

Navy had been in the office on a Sunday many times before. Managers often rated her as "devoted to her work"; friends said she was obsessive. Today the rows of empty cubicles and dark hallways seemed menacing instead of just quiet. A yellow triangle of light stretched from the partially open door of the only occupied conference room. Jackson lifted his arm from her shoulders as they turned the corner.

It wasn't a secret they were together, but they tried not to call attention to it at work. Public displays of affection reminded people they were a couple, which reminded them of how Navy met Jackson. Jackson's mission had been sabotaged, and Navy had very nearly died so someone could cover the whole mess up.

"It's a wild goose chase," said an irate, male voice. "It's another one of her games."

The answer was too muffled for Navy to hear from twenty feet away.

"How should I know why?" the irate voice asked. "I thought we hired her so we could keep an eye on her, not so she could lead us around on a leash."

Navy planted her feet. So that's how it was. Working on the floor with all the analysts had sheltered her from the bile.

"Kevin warned us about this," Jackson whispered softly in her ear. "Let's make a good entrance." He lifted a finger to his lips, then touched her elbow to nudge her forward.

When they reached the door, he motioned for her to go in first. The irate man was in the middle of another diatribe about how she should have been indicted for treason. It was her cue. She opened the door and cleared her throat. A room full of middle-aged men in suits turned to stare at her.

The irate one stopped mid-word. He was built like a walrus, complete with a bushy beard on a broad face. She watched a deep red blush spread up his cheeks while his mouth gaped open.

"Good morning, gentlemen." She scanned the room for any familiar faces and found none. Her manager would have vouched for Navy. Maybe that's why Navy's manager wasn't here.

To her left, a man with salt-and-pepper hair stood. His long hair was pulled back in a ponytail. He had an amused smile that reached his dark blue eyes. Navy just wasn't sure what he found amusing: her discomfort or the walrus man's red face.

"Good morning, Ms. Trent. My name is Saul, I got your message on Saturday." He pointed to the man who had been declaring Navy guilty. "This is Peter. He's leading our red team on this."

Navy nodded. Of course they were using a red team. It made sense. Her reports were regularly subject to red team analysis, and she had been on red teams herself. Bringing in a skeptical eye was a good way to test your theories. Except this time it wasn't a theory she was defending. It was her reputation.

Saul pulled out the only two chairs left in the room. "Please, sit."

"Thank you." The swivel chair made it easy to fidget. She scooted closer to the table and held herself still. No one would trust her if she couldn't control her nerves. She didn't dare look at Jackson for support. It would be taken as a sign of weakness.

"We should start with introductions." Saul pointed to himself. "As I said, I'm with Defections. I think we all know Ms. Trent."

His smile didn't slip, but his tone left her unsure what he thought of her.

"To Ms. Trent's right," Saul continued, "is the storied Jackson Fletcher, one of our best undercover operatives."

"Her bodyguard," someone muttered.

Saul's eyes narrowed as he scanned the room. "Let's use our manners, children. And maybe we can all get home in time for Sunday dinner."

The silence settled uncomfortably on Navy's shoulders. Part of her wished she hadn't decrypted the message at all. Part of her wondered if they were wasting time coddling egos while a desperate man waited for his chance to escape.

"That's better," Saul said. "Next to Jackson we have our North Korean experts, Uri and Eli."

Uri wore a brown suit; Eli wore a blue one. Aside from the color of the suits, Navy couldn't tell them apart. Both had pronounced brow lines and curly blond hair, cut short. Both wore glasses with thick, black frames. They nodded curtly to her, in sync.

"On the other side of the table, we have one of my colleagues from Defections, Fred."

Fred looked ten years too young for the paisley bow tie at his throat. Beneath pale green eyes, a close-cut, meticulously groomed beard covered his cheeks.

Saul waved his hand dismissively at the remaining three men. "And the rest of Peter's team."

She wondered if not introducing her would-be interrogators was a deliberate attempt to make her nervous.

Using a small white remote, Saul turned on the projector. The whine of its fan was the only sound in the room. Peter was still glaring at her. The bulb flickered on and a screen at the front of the room filled with blue. Saul reached for his laptop just as the door opened, and Kevin appeared.

Saul's ponytail flicked toward the wall as he turned his head. "Kevin?"

Kevin smiled his trademark fuck-you smile. "You didn't invite me." Today, Navy was glad to see Kevin. He had sharp blue eyes and blond hair that refused any part. He was long in all four limbs and, as she had learned in the field, deadly in knife fights or hand-to-hand combat.

"Because you don't need to be here. I shouldn't even let Jackson be here."

Jackson squeezed Navy's knee under the table. She moved her hand to meet his, grateful for the support.

"I'm her handler," Kevin said. "I need to be here."

Peter laughed harshly. "You're Jackson's handler. She doesn't have a handler; she's not a field agent."

"I ran her last year in Romania," Kevin countered.

Saul looked at his watch, annoyed. "For one mission. Her first, and last, planned undercover mission, as far as I know."

"Doesn't matter. I was her handler on that mission, and she did her work well and loyally. I'm here to make sure no one forgets that." Kevin crossed his arms and leaned against the wall, daring anyone to kick him out.

Saul pressed his lips together. "Fine. Whatever. I'd like to finish this, if you don't mind." He pointed to the image on the projector screen. "Navy, walk us through what you found and how you found it."

She swallowed over the lump in her throat. "Our IDS detected—"

"What's an IDS?" Peter asked. His tone was still combative, like she'd been deliberately hiding something.

"Pretend you're trying to explain something to me," Jackson said. His face was neutral, but his hand tightened on hers underneath the table.

One deep breath in. One deep breath out. "Our IDS—intrusion detection system—alerted on some unusual network activity targeting the payroll server. The signature matched activity generated by the PoisonIvy RAT—remote access trojan. A RAT is malware used to control a system remotely." She paused to give anyone time to contradict her or ask questions.

The twins' faces were blank, a little bored, she guessed. Peter looked like he was thinking hard, but didn't say anything. Fred adjusted his bowtie.

"The internal security team investigated the compromise and found several odd things. First, the attacker was sophisticated enough to leave no traces of activity at the border of our network but didn't bother to hide evidence on the payroll server itself."

"On what evidence do you base those conclusions?" Peter asked.

She took another deep breath, thankful for her training in meditation. "This is what I was told by our security team when they sent the file—the image of my face—over to me. But to get to the payroll server, the attacker had to go through our bastion hosts. We have gaps in those logs, indicating the attacker successfully hid their login activity. The second odd thing is that the attacker planted a remote access trojan but configured the tool with a C2 that was an RFC1918 address."

Saul looked baffled.

There was a reason Navy preferred working with machines over people. "Okay, I'll back up. Remote access trojans always phone home to a command and control—C2—address to get orders. In this case, PoisonIvy was installed and told to get its orders from an IP address that, for all practical purposes, doesn't exist."

"You're being evasive," Peter said. "What do you mean by 'for all practical purposes'"?

"I'm not—" She wasn't trying to hide information. She didn't want to explain RFC1918 to a bunch of people who couldn't even name one layer of the OSI network stack. "The C2 IP address was in RFC1918 space. Those addressees are reserved for internal network use. So PoisonIvy was told to communicate with an IP address inside our network." Peter opened his mouth to speak, and she held up her hand. "And, in some cases, that means the attacker set up a C2 server inside the network. But in this case, the internal security team found the C2 IP address had never sent a packet on our network." She chewed on her lip, trying to think of a way to make it clearer. "We keep network flows, records of network activity, for years. And there's no evidence that the C2 IP address was ever live on our network at any time during the past five years. So someone broke into our network, got to the crown jewels, then installed a malicious program and pointed it to a C2 that doesn't exist."

Now everyone's face was blank.

Time to try again. "The attacker could have walked away with our entire payroll database. She didn't."

A hint of a smile played on Saul's lips. "She?"

"Yes, she," Navy answered. "Since we don't know."

"He," corrected Uri. "If the message is genuine. Min Gyu is a male name."

Eli nodded.

"It's nice that you agree on something," Saul said.

Navy looked at Saul for permission to continue. At his nod, she spoke again. "The PoisonIvy RAT was installed just to get our attention. It never did any damage. Just to be clear, all of this investigation happened before I got involved."

"So how did you get involved?" Saul asked.

She looked at the picture of her face on the projector screen. The image was larger than life, distorted by the message hidden inside. "The attacker left the image you see on the screen inside the same directory as the PoisonIvy install. The internal security team analyzed the file on their own and couldn't find anything useful. They asked me to look at the file since it seemed to be addressed to me."

"Maybe you left it as a calling card," Peter said. "You have the skills to do this."

Navy felt Jackson lift a quarter-inch out of his chair, before a look from Kevin warned him to sit down again.

Her specialty was defensive security, not offensive. But she had written malware before, and she knew how to hide her tracks. "I didn't," she said simply.

"Prove it."

She reached for that calm place she found in her meditation sessions, the place where she was confident in her strength. "I can't." She met Peter's hostile gaze with equanimity. "The security team wasn't able to determine the full timeline of the attack, therefore I can't provide you with an alibi."

"Let's save the analysis until we've laid out all the cards," Saul said. "Finish your walk-through, Navy."

"The distortion in the image made it obvious data was hidden inside. See that red pixel in the hair on the corner? And how the shadows seem odd around the nose?" Her hair, her nose, her face. If this was some sort of trick, she would track down the person who made it. Having her name dragged through the mud once was enough. "I ran it through several steganography programs and eventually found a message encrypted with my public PGP key."

"Public key?" Saul asked.

Another complicated explanation Navy didn't want to give. "PGP is an asymmetric encryption algorithm. Asymmetric encryption means that keys come in pairs – a message encrypted with the public key can only be decrypted with my private key and vice versa. The attacker left a message that only I could have decoded."

"Which you could have done yourself," Peter said.

"My public key is available to anyone. So, yes."

"I don't think Navy left the message," Kevin said.

Peter snorted. "How surprising."

"When we discussed it, Navy didn't know what the furniture factory was."

Saul's eyes narrowed. "You discussed this with her before she came here?"

Kevin didn't back down. "Because I'm her h—"

"Handler. Right. Whatever." Saul shook his head and advanced to the next image. The message from Min Gyu appeared on the screen. "Please verify this is the message you found in the image."

`My name is Kor Min Gyu, or Min Gyu Kor as you would say in the West. I work in Office 91. I want to defect. I can destroy the furniture factory. Email and PGP key follow this message.`

The message was no less chilling to read the second time around. "Yes," she said. "That's it."

Peter opened his mouth to speak, but Fred held up a manicured hand. "We have more material to review. I asked Uri and Eli to pull some background information for us. I added the slides to your deck, Saul."

Saul handed his laptop across the table to Eli with the blue suit.

25

The screen switched to a grainy snapshot of an Asian man smiling nervously for the camera. He was sitting at a table scattered with computer parts. The motherboard looked like no board Navy had ever seen before. It was separated into squares no larger than a paper napkin. And instead of a floppy drive, there was a place to insert a VHS tape.

"We were tasked with considering the possibility the message was genuine," Eli said. "So we searched for the name in our records. This is Kor Gi Seok," said Uri. "Min Gyu's father. He was one of ours."

Even Peter seemed surprised. "Where was this picture taken? When?" he demanded.

"1990. Just across the border in China," Uri answered. "Gi Seok worked deals with the Chinese government, negotiating food in return for joint mining operations in North Korea. He had a travel pass from North Korea that made him a good candidate."

"What kind of computer is he assembling? And is that a VHS deck?" Navy couldn't resist asking.

Kevin caught her eye and shook his head slightly. "Disengage," he mouthed.

"It's mostly stock parts," Eli said. "Except for the motherboard. Techs designed the motherboard so it could be smuggled in piece by piece. The sections connect using those black cables you see dangling from the sides. In this picture, he's practicing the assembly."

"Kor Gi Seok smuggled the computer into North Korea, one part at a time," Uri continued. "The computer was used to write encrypted reports about daily life to VHS tapes, and occasionally to read tapes we gave him. With the encryption, if anyone caught him with the tapes and played them, it looked like a blank VHS."

"We invented a new computer for this guy so we could read his diary?" Peter asked.

"You have to understand that life essentially stopped in North Korea at the end of the Korean War," Eli said. "Very few people are allowed in or out. Very few people have access to media that's not controlled by the government. North Korean defectors have to relearn parts of their native tongue because the language has diverged in South Korea. North Koreans look different because of a low-quality, unreliable food supply. Every single North Korean has a file that traces their lineage back three generations to enable the collective punishment of entire families. The government has rewritten history for their population. According to them, we started the Korean War. We had an easier time getting spies into Russia than we've had getting spies into North Korea. We needed day-to-day information."

"And there was the brother," Uri said.

Eli shrugged. "Allegedly."

"Would you care to explain?" Saul asked.

"Min Gyu's uncle," Uri said. "Gi Seok, Min Gyu's father, claimed his brother, Min Gyu's uncle, was high up in the Kim hierarchy. As high as you could go without being one of the Dear Leader's bastard sons or a family member."

"He means that literally," Eli cut in. "The Dear Leader had a number of unacknowledged children who were given preferential treatment."

"Supposedly, Min Gyu's uncle was a director in weapons research," Uri continued. "We never received adequate confirmation. All we know is Gi Seok claimed that his brother was Kor Sung Yong. And other intelligence indicates there was a Kor Sung Yong in the military at that level."

"The furniture factory," Navy heard herself say.

Uri nodded. "Exactly. If Min Gyu is the actual author of this message, there's reason to believe he has contact with someone who may have been involved in the research for their nuclear weapons program."

"Kor is a common family name in North Korea," Eli said. "He could have been exaggerating his access as a bargaining chip."

"Were these files you looked at hard copy or scanned in?" asked Peter.

Uri and Eli shared a confused look. "A little of both," Uri said.

"So little miss hacker here could have pulled Min Gyu's name from the archives."

This time it was Navy's hand pressing down that kept Jackson from moving. Even Kevin looked like he might lose his cool.

"Let's leave the editorializing out of your questions, Peter. We're all aware of your theory. You can put it in your report." Saul rubbed his forehead. "Uri, Eli, what does Gi Seok's diary have to say about his son's loyalties?"

"We don't know," Uri said. "Min Gyu would have been a teenager at the time. His handler didn't push for details like that. And the reports ended in 1995. Min Gyu would be thirty-five now, if he's alive."

"If?" Peter asked.

Eli cleared his throat. "Gi Seok's body was placed at the location where his handler was supposed to meet him. He wasn't killed there. *He was placed there.* Someone wanted us to know he was dead. We lost another asset around the same time. The working theory is that Gi Seok was compromised and gave up the name of the other asset."

"*A* working theory," Uri corrected. "North Korea trumpets every victory over the West that it can. When they captured the *USS Pueblo* in 1968, they made it a fucking museum. If they'd found an American spy, with equipment proving information was being smuggled outside the country, they would have announced something, at least internally. But none of our other assets mentioned news like that."

"What's your working theory, then?" Eli asked. "Gi Seok was mugged on a business trip and they just happened to hide his body in the place where we expected to meet him?"

"My working theory is that we're missing something important." Uri leaned back and formed a triangle with his hands. "Collective punishment is the norm in North Korea. If Gi Seok was outed as a traitor, his whole family would have been sent to a prison camp. And State Security would have made sure everyone on the block knew it. But we have reports from another asset who lived on the same block as Gi Seok, detailing every family 'resettled' by State Security from 1991 to 2000. That asset says it wasn't State Security that emptied Gi Seok's house. The mother walks to work one day and never comes back, then a high-ranking military official shows up, gives the son, Min Gyu, a hug and takes him away."

"So they took one family quietly," Eli said. "Weirder things have happened."

Uri shook his head. "What about Kor Sung Yong, the uncle? Our latest intel, as of last week, confirms that a Kor Sung Yong still works in their weapons program. He never would have been able to keep that job if his brother was a traitor."

Saul was scribbling notes down as fast as he could.

"Alleged uncle," Eli said. "You said yourself that it was never adequately confirmed."

"But if it's true!" Uri said. "If it's true, the high-ranking military official that took Min Gyu away after his mother disappeared is Kor Sung Yong. And Min Gyu spent the last twenty years even closer to the furniture factory than his father was."

"Even assuming you're right, that doesn't mean Min Gyu's loyalties are in the right place," Eli said. "If he's been raised by a true believer since the age of fifteen, he's probably brainwashed. And there's nothing to prove the message is even from him. Maybe State Security is using the name because they know we know it."

Navy was always amazed by how complicated analyzing intelligence reports could be. Most days it made her job interesting and exciting. Today the stakes were more personal, and she wished the dueling twins could make up their minds.

The tapping of Saul's pen measured the silence. "So, to sum up. Either the message was faked by Navy herself, or it was faked by State Security, or the message is from Min Gyu and he wants to help, or the message is from Min Gyu and he wants to kill more evil American bastards."

Uri and Eli nodded. "Exactly," they both said at the same time.

"Occam's razor," Peter said. "The simplest explanation is often the correct one."

Kevin's eyes narrowed. "What was your role in CRYSTAL again?"

"Not everyone in the room is cleared to talk about CRYSTAL." Peter stood, gathering his notepad and papers studiously.

"There was a series of articles on the front page of the *New York Times*," Kevin said. "Let's not play pretend. I think you were even mentioned in one of them. Not by name, of course. They used your nickname, Shepherd."

Peter's chair slammed against the table when he pushed it in. "I was an analyst for the CRYSTAL project."

"Is this really ne—" Saul started but Kevin spoke over him.

"And do you remember why they called you Shepherd?" Kevin asked. "You cried wolf so many times your director had to review all your reports."

"It wasn't my fault," Peter said, subdued. "The program was flawed."

"Yeah, it was. But instead of pointing that out, you kept on generating reports that sent my agents on wild goose chases in dangerous parts of the world. You should be thanking Navy. She probably saved your goddamn career by killing that project."

Instead of cowing Peter, the comment reanimated him. "She wrote a virus that revealed the existence and details of a top secret project, and you're defending her? There are right ways and wrong ways to solve a problem, you know that."

Kevin had told her to not make waves, but Navy was tired of letting other people do her fighting. She stood up and kept a hand on Jackson's shoulder to make sure he didn't. "Letting them kill me wouldn't have stopped the leak. And they would have gone after my friends. I had no choice." The emotion in her voice surprised her.

Peter's head jerked her way. "That's an excuse—"

"You read the reports. You know everything I did and why I did it. What would you have done?"

"Something else," he snapped.

"Children, *please*," Saul said as he closed his laptop. "Peter, I'll expect your team's initial report on my desk tomorrow morning. Uri and Eli, the same for you. You are all dismissed. Navy, Jackson, and Kevin can stay a minute."

Inwardly, Navy sighed. Kevin had been right. She should have kept her mouth shut. At least the only person left to see her dressing-down was Fred, Saul's coworker from Defections.

Saul stood and tucked his laptop and files under one arm. "Navy, I want you out of this process as soon as possible."

Relief deflated her stiff posture. "You don't think I faked the message from Min Gyu."

"It doesn't matter whether or not I believe you. If the message is real, this is big. We have to attempt to make contact. And your presence is distracting my team. I need alternate theories, not Peter's recycled diatribes."

Out of the corner of her eye, she saw Kevin hide a smile. So that had been his plan all along. Kevin's emotional outburst was a strategic move to discredit her most vocal critic. She straightened, hoping she looked more confident than she felt. "I would like nothing more than to be done with this."

"Good. We're in agreement then. I'll notify you when we make contact. When we do, you will be put in an isolation room with Fred until this guy returns our email or until my hair finishes turning gray."

On either side of her, she felt Jackson and Kevin relax. This was the out she wanted. And she couldn't take it, even though she knew where her question would lead. "How are you going to email him?"

Saul scowled. "With the help of my techs. Using my keyboard. Encrypted with . . . the key or whatever for the email address he gave us."

Navy chose her next words carefully. "If you send him an email encrypted only with his public key, Min Gyu won't know who sent the message."

Saul looked at her blankly.

"Anyone can encrypt a message using Min Gyu's public key. You have to send a message that could only come from us."

"So I'll set up my own address on some free email service and get my own key," Saul said. "And then, publish that key? However you published yours."

"I—" Navy took a deep breath. "How will Min Gyu know that the email is a CIA contact? And if you send the email from an official CIA account, you might as well turn in Min Gyu yourself."

Saul spoke through his teeth. "So if I can't send the email from a CIA account and I can't send it from a non-CIA account, how should I send it?"

Navy shifted slightly so she couldn't see Kevin's glare. Her next words would make no one happy. "You have to send it from a non-CIA account. Encrypted with my private key. That's what he's expecting."

Fred shrugged. "Easy enough. Give us your private key then."

The ventilation system kicked on with a loud hum. She felt every wisp of air against her skin. "I can't."

"Navy." Kevin's whisper was sharp and ominous.

She backed away from everyone. "The point of a private key is that it belongs to one person. Me. My key has been signed by friends and past coworkers. This isn't just about me. There's a web of trust. If I give my private key to anyone, I violate that trust."

Jackson looked nearly as angry as Kevin. Saul hadn't calmed down either. "You're telling me that you have to read the message we send to Min Gyu."

Finally, she could give an answer she was happy about. "No, we can encrypt it twice. Once with a key of your choosing, then I can add a message pointing him to that public key and encrypt it with my key. That way we can establish a channel of communication that doesn't include me."

Saul's pen tapped-tapped-tapped against his files. "Fine. Then you're out."

"Gladly," she said.

Chapter 5

Manicured lawns and picture-perfect houses traveled past Erin's car windows. Children watched by attentive parents played on plastic trikes in driveways. Every scene was a postcard of the white-picket-fence life that everyone was supposed to aspire to. If she lived here, Erin thought, she'd die of boredom. She was here for a social call, or as close as she ever came to a social call.

Once a year, Byron's family threw a party and invited everyone they knew. This year, she could see, there was even a bright red bouncy castle with yellow turrets surrounded by a crowd of excited children. The party was a good cover for the annual ritual she and Jackson shared with Byron.

As she parked her car behind the line of cars near Byron's house, she saw Jackson and Navy on the lawn. Navy was deep in conversation with Byron's daughter, Clara, near the castle. Byron looked every bit the proud suburban dad with a short-sleeve polo shirt, khaki pants, and a hint of a gut protruding over his belt. Erin didn't let the soft image deceive her. Byron didn't have the temperament for fieldwork, but he had the skills.

Erin pasted on her best smile to prepare for her entrance. She might as well be under deep cover here. She didn't have children; she didn't want any. She didn't have a house because she preferred to move often. She didn't have a mower, a snow blower, a vegetable garden, or opinions on home decorating. Her hobbies all involved shooting things. Her job involved a lot of that too. Technically, her title was the same as Jackson's. They were both undercover field agents. The difference was that people the CIA didn't like had a habit of dying when she was around.

Jackson waved when he saw Erin step into the yard. Navy turned and smiled at her. Navy was not the sort of friend Erin had ever imagined having. Navy was normal. No, Erin corrected herself, Navy had certain skills that not everyone had. And she had, by choice, avoided the entanglements of marriage and children just as Erin had. But somehow Navy managed to walk in both worlds: the world of guns and knives and secrets and the normal world of mortgages and potty training.

The wind stirred and the first of the fall leaves twirled down from the oak in Byron's yard. In a couple weeks, people would be digging coats out of the back of their closets and searching for last year's gloves. Erin would, hopefully, be on her next assignment. She took a beer from the bucket full of ice and filled a plate with dip and vegetables. Munching was always a good excuse to let someone else carry the conversation.

Out of habit, she eavesdropped on the conversations as she weaved through the crowd toward Navy. Two women sharing complaints about their nannies. Couples sharing tips for easy worknight dinners. Because of her training, the useless information would be stuck in her head for days.

"They told me you would show up," Navy said. "But I didn't believe it."

Erin raised her beer and one eyebrow. "To faking it."

The green bottles clinked. A troubled look passed across Navy's face before her smile reappeared. "To faking it."

Perhaps the dust-up with the North Korean defector was worrying Navy, Erin thought. Erin knew Jackson was worried, and for good reason. The last thing Navy needed was to attract more attention.

"Erin, good to see you. Glad you could make it." Byron slapped her on the shoulder, as close to a hug as Erin would allow.

Clara, Byron's daughter, was pulled into the bouncy castle by her friends. Byron had a nostalgic smile as he watched the college sophomore go.

"I can see why you're proud," Jackson said. "She's done well."

"Am I that obvious?" Byron asked.

"It's adorable," Navy assured him. "And last year was a close call."

Navy was referring to Clara's brush with a Romanian human trafficking gang. The contact that led to Navy going undercover.

"I like to pretend that didn't happen," Byron said.

"What did you tell her about why Andrei disappeared?" Jackson asked.

Byron glanced at Navy, surprised. "Navy didn't tell you? She spoofed an email from Andrei saying he was getting back together with his high school sweetheart. Clara cursed his name for a month. It was music to my ears."

"It's probably better that way," Jackson said.

The truth was that Andrei had been beaten to death when his boss learned he was trying to leave.

"Byron's study in twenty?" Erin asked. Twenty minutes of miserable small talk should be enough to make it look like she wasn't here just to see Byron and Jackson.

Byron nodded. "I hid the good scotch. If you find it, you can take the bottle home."

Navy looked confused. "We're having an adult Easter egg hunt?"

"Just the three of us." Jackson gestured between himself, Byron, and Erin. "Nothing for you to worry about. I'll explain later."

"Honey," called Byron's wife from across the lawn. "We need more beer in the cooler."

"Duty calls," Byron said as he walked away.

Jackson's attention was on a man standing near Byron's front door. About the same age as Jackson, mid-thirties, with an athletic build and close-cropped brown hair.

"I see an old army buddy." Jackson kissed Navy on the cheek. "See you after the Easter egg hunt."

The opening Jackson left was soon filled by a plump older woman with fine blond hair sprayed into submission. "I don't mean to be rude, but are you two sisters? My sister and I couldn't help but notice how much you two look alike."

Erin rejected all the phrases that immediately came to her mind, hoping Navy would answer. When Navy didn't, Erin slipped back into her cover. "We get that all the time! I'm Erin." For good measure, Erin stuck out her hand.

A cloud of perfume followed the woman's hand. Erin placed it immediately. A mid-range perfume sold at most department stores. That and the woman's clothes, placed her income in the lower-middle-class range. Her hairstyle was ten years out of fashion, which meant she was likely a traditionalist. Her wedding ring was garish, though probably real. Her politics probably ran right of center.

Erin took note of all these things in the time it took the woman to say, "I'm Sylvia."

Sylvia waved her sister over and for the next ten minutes Erin learned more than she ever wanted to know about collectible Beanie Babies. The conversation ended with a squeal when Sylvia noticed her neighbor arriving at the party. The high-pitched yells coming from the bouncy castle were making Erin twitch. She steered Navy to a cluster of tables on the other side of the lawn.

Erin righted one of the folding chairs next to a card table and sat down. On this side of the lawn, the din was from the combined conversations of all the happy, smiling people crowding Byron's lawn. Erin wouldn't admit to jealousy.

Most of them were faking it anyway. She had been an uninvited guest in enough homes to know that.

Navy took the seat next to Erin. There were definitely bags under Navy's eyes.

"What's your apartment like?" Navy asked.

Erin took a long pull of her beer. "That's a little out of the blue."

"I was just thinking that I've seen Byron's house and Jackson's apartment ... Jackson's and my apartment now, I guess. But when you and I get together, it's always at a bar or restaurant."

The question felt as intimate as asking for a look in her underwear drawer. "It's a downtown DC apartment. Small and expensive."

Navy smiled her first genuine smile of the day. "My question bothers you. Never mind."

Out of habit, Erin scanned the faces in the crowd in front of her. Maybe there was some genuine happiness there. Maybe connecting with people wasn't so terrible. "Page 98."

Navy looked confused.

"Page 98 of the Ikea catalog. That's what my apartment looks like." Erin glanced at her watch and saw what she was hoping for, an easy out. "Time for the Easter egg hunt."

She tossed her beer in the garbage can brimming with other bottles, then slipped around the back of the house. The relative quiet was a relief to her ears. In the back door, down the stairs, and to the left. The annual ritual was comforting. Jackson and Byron already had the scotch out, ruining her fun. They poured her a glass without asking.

"Sorry I'm late," Erin said. "I was having a heart-to-heart with Navy."

Byron looked dubious. He handed her a glass. All three raised their drinks in a silent toast. Words would have cheapened the moment. It was a recognition of their friendship, yes, but also a recognition of how quickly forces outside these walls could test that bond—or sever it. Undercover work was dangerous. That was part of its charm.

Jackson pulled two key rings from his pocket and handed one to Erin and Byron. "The larger key is for a public storage unit 32 in Bailey's Crossroads. The code to the main door is 49283. Don't trip over Buck."

Buck was Jackson's less-than-imaginative name for the mounted deer head that formed the cover for the unit. Anyone discovering the collection of guns, taxidermy, and nonperishable food would assume the unit belonged to a hunter. The cash stored inside Buck would be a little harder to explain. Every cache included food, guns, and cash.

"The smaller key is a mailbox at the Mail 'n' More nearby," Jackson continued. "Box 78 is rented under the names Bill and Mary Revere."

To aid in the memorization, Erin pulled up the image of the last public storage building she'd been in. She imagined walking up to a barred door with a keypad and typing in the code 4-9-2-8-3. She imagined walking down a hallway, following the numbers. 25, 27, 29 on one side, 26, 28, 30 on the other. Until she reached unit 32, where she put the key in the lock and opened the door to a collection of animals with glassy, unblinking eyes. Buck, she imagined, was a ten-point buck with tan fur and a black nose. His tapered mouth opened and said, "Bailey's Crossing, Mail 'n' More, Box 78."

She did the exercise a couple more times, varying the order of the information in her walkthrough, until she was satisfied. Byron would be using his own tricks for memorization.

Jackson waited patiently. His turn would come soon.

Erin and Byron looked up at the same time and nodded to each other. It was her signal to go. She pulled out two key rings and handed one to Byron, one to Jackson.

"Number 8 at the Coral Hills Courtyard Office Suites. The key will get you in the front door and the office door. Cash and guns are in the safe, combination 34-21-89-50. Snacks in the desk drawers."

Erin paused to let them process, then continued. "Dead drop location is the coffee shop bathroom across the street. There's a Maneki Neko on a shelf. One of those cats that waves, except this one is just a statue. It's hollow. Leave the message inside."

She waited while Byron and Jackson memorized the details. The caches and dead drop locations were contingency plans. They had disposable phones with numbers shared only between themselves, but they needed a way to contact each other if even those channels failed. And supplies in case someone needed to leave the country quickly. In her business, she could never be too careful. Most recently, they had used their contingency plans when they needed to rescue Navy from their own agency.

On Byron's turn, he rattled off another public storage location and another rented mailbox, which she duly memorized. Then, with another silent toast, they separated.

Erin left the party without saying goodbye to Navy. Erin was sure Navy would understand. Sometimes pretending to be good and normal was just too much.

Chapter 6

Friday morning. Young Sun, his coworker, was in the office early again. Min Gyu had been hoping to have the office to himself. Today was his last chance to check email until Monday. He forced himself to set up his defenses slowly and carefully. Fake enough legitimate traffic for Mirage to record and then replay. *Don't get caught now.* Ten minutes later, he checked the email address he'd given Navy, expecting to be disappointed again. Instead he saw: "Furniture order confirmation."

He heard himself gasp and covered it with a cough. Young Sun looked up, annoyed, then back to his terminal. The email text could have been spam, but the attachment looked like gibberish. Encrypted.

Navy's public key decrypted the file. There were two parts, a text file and another file that appeared to be encrypted. He hesitated before opening the text message. The answer could be no. After all, the U.S. had their own cyber warriors better trained and better equipped than he was. The answer could be an apology for her inability to help. Seconds rolled by on his clock, ticking off the precious ten minutes of cover Mirage gave him.

Hold your back straight, Min Gyu told himself. Like your father taught you. Whatever the answer was, Min Gyu could not afford to show a reaction. *Decrypt the message already*, he told himself.

```
We are interested. Write something to
prove you are who you say you are.
Encrypted message is from your new
handler. Communicate directly with him
from now on. Email follows this message.
```

Public key on MIT PGP key server. Leave me out of it.

Odd that she seemed so hostile. But the answer wasn't no. He pulled down the key for his handler and decrypted the second message. This one was less hostile.

We are eager to discuss your proposal but require further proof. Please send the full details of your plan. If you can do what you promise, we will make arrangements.

Less hostile, but less trustworthy too. Min Gyu didn't trust them not to steal his plan and leave him to rot. He considered Navy's message again. She was direct, rude even. But even her worst critics had never accused her of being a liar. A traitor, yes. A dangerous idealist too focused on the value of individual rights. But never dishonest. He would prove who he was. He would give them a few details, but not enough they could burn down the furniture factory without him. He would press that button when he was safe across the ocean.

The format of his reply mimicked theirs, an encrypted message within an encrypted message. One message to tell his handler he would only talk through Navy. Another, encrypted with Navy's public key, providing all the information they needed. Now he just had to survive the rest of the day.

His fellow cyber warriors arrived quietly, then set to work clicking at their keyboards. The good news should have left him elated. Instead, he spent the day watching the time pass with agonizing slowness. Plus, tonight was the dreaded family dinner.

Leaving early wasn't going to earn him any brownie points, but as with most decisions in North Korea, he had to choose between bad and worse. Bad—reminding his superior officer that Min Gyu's family had more status by accepting a dinner invitation from Min Gyu's uncle, the director of nuclear weapons research. On Monday, Min Gyu would be assigned some disagreeable, but supposedly honorary, task in return. Worse—turning down an invitation from Kor Sung Yong that Min Gyu had accepted with regularity for eight years, since he started his job in Office 91. Back when he still believed.

 He logged out of his terminal and shrugged into his uniform jacket. It was exactly ten strides to his superior's office. Through the narrow pane of glass in the door, he saw his superior glance up at him, then back to his keyboard. Forcing Min Gyu to interrupt him was part of their weekly apology ritual. The metal door was cold on Min Gyu's knuckles.

 Commander Jang Dae Won looked up with a sour expression. "Please come in."

 "Honorable Commander Jang," Min Gyu said with a slight bow. "My uncle has requested a consultation regarding network security this afternoon."

 "As he does most Friday afternoons," Dae Won noted.

 "He takes his job very seriously. My apologies for the interruption in my work."

 "No one has looked at honeypot logs for two weeks. I was hoping you could do that today." Honeypots were servers set up to be deliberately insecure, to tempt attackers to reveal their tactics. Reviewing the logs meant hours of sorting through script kiddy activity, just for the unlikely prize of a new sophisticated attack.

 Min Gyu kept his expression neutral, prepared for the next step in this dance. "I will work tomorrow to catch up on those tasks." His network activity was monitored in near-real time. That's what his commander did most of the day. Min Gyu happened to know a big celebration was planned for Saturday at one of the Great Leader's villas. Anyone high-ranking enough to watch Min Gyu would want to be there.

"That won't be necessary." Dae Won hid a glare behind his false smile. "Your devotion to your family is honorable."

"I humbly try to follow the example of our Great Leader and be a servant to our people." A bit over the top perhaps, but Min Gyu had so few opportunities to have fun.

"Please send greetings to your uncle," Dae Won said. "You are dismissed."

Min Gyu took the stairs. The elevator had been broken for a year. Even maintaining the building for the elite cyber corps took a back seat to the main priority of every North Korean citizen: the fervent admiration of the Supreme Leader Kim Jong Eun. That meant spending less money for functioning elevators and more money on lavish celebrations like the party on Saturday. Min Gyu knew about the event because his uncle would be there, and next week his uncle would gleefully share the details with Min Gyu.

Min Gyu could probably recite the details himself by now, even though he'd never been. The parties were all the same. There would be mountains of food and unlimited alcohol, and when those appetites were satisfied, the Happy Corps girls. The girls were trained specifically for the pleasure of Kim Jong Eun. Other cadres of girls were trained more generally and available to men like his uncle.

As Min Gyu reached the lobby, he could see the limo, one of the many perks available to his uncle. The car was idling outside the front door, clearly audible in the lobby. Min Gyu tried to imagine what it would be like to live in a normal place. Like New York City, maybe. Where the streets were full of cars, as streets should be.

The limo sat like a black beetle next to the curb. Min Gyu had to force himself to keep walking. Once, he had loved his uncle. Now, he couldn't think of anyone he hated more. The driver of the limo scrambled out to open the back door for Min Gyu. A new driver this week. Sung Yong went through drivers quickly. His temper was legendary, but he was smart enough to take it out on people ranked below him.

Min Gyu slipped into the sleek interior, nearly wrinkling his nose at the new-car smell. The car wasn't new. Very few in North Korea were. But his uncle liked to use air fresheners that mimicked the aroma of fresh plastic.

"My son." Sung Yong opened his arms and waited for Min Gyu to hug him.

Min Gyu bit the inside of his cheek and tasted blood. Revenge would come later. For now, he had to be the good son. "I have missed you, Uncle."

When they separated, Sung Yong rubbed his hands together like an overgrown child. "Did you bring it?"

The thumb drive in Min Gyu's pocket could easily get him killed. If he was ever found with it, he doubted Sung Yong's paternal instincts would extend to admitting the pirated South Korean dramas were downloaded at his request. But Sung Yong's indulgence was an easy opportunity to get malware into the furniture factory. After all, the best place to watch illicit videos was in your office with the door closed. Even Sung Yong wasn't allowed to have a computer at home. When it became clear how the furniture factory had been infected—and it would be clear—Sung Yong would be taken to one of the dark, bloody rooms where such things were settled.

He would break quickly under torture, Min Gyu imagined, though he hoped otherwise. Sung Yong should suffer like Min Gyu's mother had suffered.

Min Gyu handed the thumb drive to his loving, duplicitous uncle and sat back against the seat. The ride to the enclave was blessedly short. Min Gyu could have walked it. But Sung Yong liked to be seen with Min Gyu. Sung Yong wanted all his neighbors to know that he had raised one of the country's prized cyber warriors.

Sung Yong's apartment was in one of the special enclaves reserved for high-ranking officials in the government. If you forgot that every official was a hair's breadth away from being executed if they fell under suspicion, and that every room was bugged, it was a wonderful place to live. The high-rise building was on the official route for the surprisingly regular tour buses in the city. Min Gyu couldn't understand why there were so many people willing to be tourists in North Korea. They were shown only what minders wanted them to see. In some government buildings, their cameras were taken because pictures were forbidden. A good opportunity, no doubt, for someone to review the pictures that had been taken.

The limo turned into a parking garage underneath the gleaming white building. There were plenty of others like it parked in the numbered spots. The driver stopped near the door to the elevator lobby, then ran to open the door for Sung Yong. Min Gyu let himself out.

In the elevator lobby, the floor tiles were spotless. Min Gyu could still smell the sharp tang of disinfectant in the air. Elevator rides made him nervous. Appearance was always more important than functionality in buildings like this. Not that his uncle would ever lower himself to walking the stairs. He might shed that belly rounding out his uniform coat. The one that advertised his prestige and power.

"I told Kyung Ok to prepare a hanjeongsik for us." His uncle grinned like a spoiled child. "There will be so many dishes, we will be eating all night."

Min Gyu forced a smile. It wasn't the thought of food that was twisting his stomach. Kyung Ok, his uncle's wife, was a good cook. It was the idea of sitting in *that* apartment again. The apartment where Min Gyu spent his adolescence unlearning everything his parents had taught him. The apartment where his uncle had helped him study for the university entrance exams. Even then, Min Gyu had understood it was Sung Yong's status that would get him entry to Kim Il Sung University. But Min Gyu studied diligently anyway. He had wanted to make Sung Yong proud.

The elevator shimmied and squeaked up to his uncle's floor. The hallway it opened into was unadorned. In the South Korean dramas his uncle prized so much, luxury apartment buildings had art and doormen and fancy carpet. Yes, South Korea had greater wealth disparity. But a poor person in South Korea had a better standard of life than some middle-class North Koreans. And there were no prison camps in South Korea dedicated to reeducation. Min Gyu often wondered how his uncle watched so much and understood so little.

Sung Yong did not hug or kiss his wife in greeting, but his eyes lingered on her with the affection a stable owner would have for his prize horse.

Min Gyu mumbled a greeting and quickly made his way to the table nearly covered with steaming dishes of various delicacies. There was kimchi, of course. But there was also japchae and savory pancakes and a large bowl of gomguk. The floating entrails spoke to the peasant roots of the dish. In gomguk, every edible part of the cow was used. Despite its humble origins, its presence was another marker of wealth. His uncle insisted on beef at least once a week and rice every day. Most North Koreans were lucky to get beef once a month, and ate noodles made from whatever starch was available.

"Just as I promised!" Sung Yong proclaimed. "Look at this feast Kyung Ok has prepared for us!"

Kyung Ok was much younger than his uncle and, even Min Gyu would admit, beautiful. She had a cupid bow's mouth and glistening jet-black hair. Her wide eyes were carefully outlined for effect, and always cast down in a demure fashion. The feelings she aroused in him were uncomfortable, and not just for the obvious reasons. She was a symbol of everything that was wrong in this place.

His uncle's wife had been part of the Happy Corps, the personal harem for the Supreme leader. When women in the Happy Corps reached their early twenties they were considered too old to be desirable anymore, and they were given other lives. Some, like Kyung Ok, became the wives of top officials. Some were given cushy jobs. But, regardless, Kyung Ok was desirable because that's how the regime had forced her to survive. And Min Gyu hated himself for responding to the pretense.

"Excuse me, Uncle." Min Gyu escaped down the hallway to the bathroom. But once he was out of sight, he slipped into his uncle's room. He needed a reminder of why he was risking having his fingernails torn out, one by one.

His uncle kept a jewelry box on his nightstand for his collection of portrait badges. Sung Yong had always encouraged Min Gyu to admire the collection. The jewelry box was as black as Kyung Ok's hair and shined like it had been recently cleaned. Mother of pearl inlays showed the profile of Mount Paektu, the supposed birthplace of Kim Il Sung. Cranes with wings fully spread hovered over stylized pine trees with puffs of luminescent green pearl inlays. It was constructed like a cabinet, with two doors that opened to reveal carved wooden drawers. Three of the drawers contained a collection of pins, all of which showed Kim Il Sung's face.

Every morning when he got dressed, Min Gyu had to remember to put on a pin with the unsmiling, enameled face of Kim Il Sung circled in gold. Min Gyu's badge had a simple, white background. Sung Yong's jewelry box contained an identical one. Not that his uncle would ever wear it again. Officially, the badges were supposed to be a symbol of reverence to the Great Leader. Unofficially, they were another way to mark status. Sung Yong wore a pin with Kim Il Sung's and Kim Jong Il's face against the background of a red flag, a pin befitting his status. Sung Yong kept the simpler designs in the jewelry box to chronicle his rise in the party.

The fourth drawer contained a small puzzle box, about the size of a deck of cards. Min Gyu had discovered the puzzle box the weekend before he left for Kim Il Sung University. His uncle was at one of the various party social functions where people smiled and schemed in equal parts. Kyung Ok had not been gifted to Sung Yong at that time, which left Min Gyu alone in the apartment. It had never occurred to Min Gyu that opening the puzzle box would change history as he knew it. It was a curiosity to pass the time.

A simple wooden box. A casual observer wouldn't even think it could be opened. Min Gyu weighed the rectangle in his hands. Nothing clinked inside. Its precious contents, he knew, were wrapped in a strip of cloth. The strip of cloth often made him wonder if his uncle had intended to keep the secret. Or if Min Gyu was supposed to find it someday. Min Gyu had received a similar one as a gift. Sung Yong's puzzle box, though, had a code that could be changed. And opening it required a secret word, a word his uncle assumed only had significance to himself and Min Gyu's father.

Hu-ri. A small city in South Korea whose name was often whispered around the dinner table before his parents died. Min Gyu's grandfather had been born there. He was a South Korean soldier, the sole survivor of his unit during the Korean War. To avoid capture, he'd stolen the credentials and uniform of a dead North Korean. But he'd never managed to get out of the country. Min Gyu's memories of his grandfather were indistinct, sharpened only by his father's constant stories. Stories he was told never to repeat to his uncle. Min Gyu's father had planned to escape. The whole family was going to defect. And then, one day, his father hadn't come home from a business trip. And his mother didn't come home from the factory. And his uncle had been there to give him a new home.

Min Gyu heard clinks from the kitchen. Wine glasses. Western wine, of course, because it had to be imported. Every week the same disgusting abundance that he had once reveled in. For three years after his parents died, he had been taken in by his uncle's lies. Min Gyu had abandoned his father's dreams of escape and embraced the mad logic of the Kim Jong Il regime. Until Min Gyu found this box.

Using the hidden catch, Min Gyu released the top panel. Four concentric, wooden rings of letters were visible underneath. The first dial slid smoothly to "H." Then "U." His hands were shaking. They always shook at this part. He dialed the last two letters, then lifted the strip of fabric out of the carved opening, no larger than his thumb. Two metal items winked at him under the light of the lamp on the nightstand.

He wasn't worried about his uncle interrupting him yet. Min Gyu could hear Kyung Ok's practiced giggles. That meant Sung Yong was pawing at Kyung Ok in the kitchen.

Min Gyu lifted a portrait badge out of the opening, one much like his. Except this one had been his mother's. He knew by the careful repair to the white enameled background. He had witnessed the damage. His father's ration cards should have provided them adequate rice, but food shortages meant there was sometimes no food to give out. After her third week without rice or corn, Min Gyu's mother had come home in tears, wondering how she was going to feed her family from an empty plastic bag. In the privacy of their home, she'd taken a hammer to her pin. His father had managed to stop her before the damage was irreparable. Where the white enamel had chipped, his father had used sawdust, glue, and paint to fill it in. If you didn't look closely, the repair was invisible.

The last time Min Gyu had seen his mother was when he was fifteen. She left for work in the morning and never came back. His uncle told him that she had died in an accident at the factory. If Min Gyu's mother had died in an accident at the factory, she would have been buried with the pin.

The thought of his mother's pin had festered with Min Gyu for years after he'd discovered it. Training for the cyberwar division at the university had given him access to certain records most people couldn't see. He'd used that access to comb the records for hints about his mother's disappearance. Eventually, he found a record of a thirty-five-year-old woman sent to a re-education camp who matched his mother's description. Under a different name, of course.

Some nights he fantasized that he would find her alive. Some nights he thought too much about what happened in those camps, and wished her the peace of death.

Sung Yong wouldn't be able to keep his cushy job if the government knew his sister-in-law had planned to defect. He could have made her disappear quietly and painlessly, but he didn't. He risked forging the paperwork because he wanted her punished. He knew she couldn't do anything to hurt him without also risking punishment for Min Gyu.

The second item hidden in the puzzle box was a simple scratched golden wedding ring. His father's. Min Gyu replaced both items in their hiding spot with unshaking hands, warmed by his own fury. His uncle would get what he deserved. North Korea's nuclear program might not be destroyed by Min Gyu's carefully crafted code. But his uncle would die while being tortured by the regime he loved so much. Sung Yong would beg, he would plead, he would say it wasn't his fault, and none of that would make a difference. Min Gyu heard Sung Yong's footsteps in the hallway.

"I was admiring your portrait collection, Uncle," Min Gyu said. "Please excuse me for having made you wait."

Chapter 7

When Navy stepped out of the elevator on Monday morning, she saw the last person she wanted to see. Saul stood in her cube, fingers tapping against the back of her chair. His eyes were scanning the floor. Had she missed a meeting? What could be left for her to do? She didn't know what Defections had written to Min Gyu, and she didn't care. She had encrypted the message and sent it on.

Navy almost made it into the break room without being seen when Saul spotted her.

"Navy, you're needed upstairs."

A "Good morning" wouldn't have softened the news, she supposed. "Could I get coffee first?"

Saul's narrowed eyes answered her question.

"Right. Upstairs. Got it." She dropped her bag on her chair with a sigh, grabbed her laptop, and followed Saul's salt-and-pepper ponytail to the elevators.

The room for this discussion was smaller, but no less hostile. Uri and Eli seemed angry. Kevin nodded curtly to her as she entered, clearly upset about something. Jackson wasn't there. But why would he be? This meeting hadn't been planned in advance. At least Peter wasn't here to heckle her.

"Have a seat, Navy," Saul said.

She sat on her hands to keep them still.

Saul turned his laptop and set it down in front of her. A terminal showed the commands Saul had used to decrypt the attachment on Min Gyu's email.

`I will only speak through Navy. I do not trust you.`

"You told me you wanted out," Saul said.

If she ever met Min Gyu, she would strangle him. It was bad enough he'd used her in the first place, but now it looked like she was setting herself up as the go-between. "Because that's the truth. You saw my message to him."

Eli glared at her. "Is this a joke to you? Do you read the papers at all? North Korea's nuclear weapons program is what gives them negotiating power. If North Korea couldn't flatten Seoul, we would have—"

"I'm not lying!" She hated how she sounded. Desperate and cornered. Defensive. They would never believe her if she couldn't control herself. "I swear. I'm not lying."

Kevin rubbed his forehead and sighed. "Before we finish the witch hunt, why don't we have Navy decrypt the rest of the message."

"That she could have encrypted herself," Saul said.

"Maybe there's something in the message to prove it's Min Gyu," Uri said, his eyes looking a little desperate.

Jackson's warnings were beginning to make sense now. The reputation of an analyst was only as good as their predictions. Uri's reputation was on the line now too.

"Fine. Decrypt the damn thing," Saul said. "And you better hope your imaginary friend comes through."

She opened her laptop and logged in. Saul had forwarded the message to her early that morning, while she was driving into work. Feel your breath, she told herself. Meditation had taught her to concentrate on the slight warmth of the air she released from her lungs and the cooler air that filled them. Her calm was fragile and hard-won. She still fumbled her passphrase the first time. The second time a long message appeared on her screen. She didn't waste time reading it.

Navy pointed toward the bundle of various video connectors near Saul. "May I?" A swipe of Saul's arm sent them her way. Navy prayed that something in the long

55

string of text now displayed on the wall would exonerate her.

    I am Min Gyu Kor. My father was Gi Seok Kor. We built the computer he smuggled in together. He sent you messages using VHS tapes.
    I don't know what detail will prove that you need to take me seriously. I will tell you everything I know. My mother was Ho Sook Kor. My uncle is Sung Yong Kor, director of the nuclear weapons program. My uncle killed my father when I was 15. He has my father's wedding ring. My father went on one of his business trips to China and never came back. He left me with instructions. If anything happened to him, my mother and I were supposed to get out and go to Zhenxing. His handler met him in the hotel bar at the corner of Zhenba St S and Xinger Rd every two weeks. He said his handler would help us if something happened to him. Now, I'm not so sure.
    My mother was sent to a prison camp under a different name, In Sook Kor. She is probably dead.
    My uncle loves South Korean TV shows. For several years, I have pirated them for him and put them on thumb drives. He watches them on his computer at work. This is how I was able to put malware on his computer. The malware has spread to nearly every computer on the network of machines used in our enrichment plants. It is traceable only to him. I know how far it

has spread because the malware is designed to check in every day. The check-ins are nearly undetectable on the network because the malware uses a P2P protocol.

On my signal, the malware will destroy the centrifuges and erase all electronic documents and research. Do not ask me to share this signal with you.

Uri jumped out of his seat and jabbed at a sentence with his finger. "The meeting spot! That's your proof. That wasn't in the files anywhere. Only Eli and I and his handler know that information."

A slow smile spread across Eli's face. "Congratulations, brother. You were right."

Saul looked like a kid on Christmas morning. "This means…" His hands fluttered against the table. "It's true. We can defang North Korea."

Navy let out a breath. She was cleared.

"I'm glad that's settled," Kevin said. "Now we need to get him profiled."

Saul nodded. "We need to figure out what will earn his trust. Get Navy out of the loop. But while she's here…"

Navy found all eyes in the room on her. "What?"

"The computer stuff," Kevin said. "What does it mean? He put a P2P filesharing program on his uncle's computer at work?"

The switch from pariah to technical expert left her head spinning. "Ummm, not exactly. I think he means he put P2P malware in a pirated video file. Then his uncle watched the video at work."

Kevin squinted at the screen. "And he got the file from a P2P network?"

"Maybe? He doesn't say where he got the pirated TV shows," Navy said. "He means the malware he planted uses a P2P protocol to communicate between nodes. In a highly monitored network like North Korea's, it makes it easier for the malware to fly under the radar."

Everyone's face was blank. "If every single infected computer had to call out to the C2 server, it would create more traffic," Navy said. "More of an opportunity for someone to notice what was going on. And with a single C2 server it's easier to find out how many machines are infected – just find all the machines talking to that one C2 IP address. With a P2P protocol, only a few machines need to call out. You could call them parent nodes. The rest of the infected machines can get their orders from the parent nodes."

"So he's telling the truth about what he can do?" Uri asked, his face flushed.

"Well, I don't know. Unless we see the malware itself, I can't say for sure."

Uri settled back in his chair. "That's no big deal. We'll just ask him for it."

Kevin and Saul laughed.

"You'll lose him if you do that," Kevin said. "He doesn't trust you. If you ask him to make himself irrelevant, he'll assume you're not going to give him asylum."

"Oh. Are we just going to take his word for it?" Uri asked.

"Time for Navy and me to go," Kevin said. "Call her when you need her. Share as little information with her as possible. You know the drill."

Navy scrambled to close her computer and push her chair back.

In the hallway, Kevin steered her toward the elevators. "Coffee? I know this great place just around the block."

"Actually, I'd kind of like to get to my real w—"

Kevin shook his head. "No, you want coffee." Someone came into view and Kevin smiled with forced cheerfulness. "Good coffee. The stuff here is terrible."

His tone made it clear she didn't have a choice. She followed him out of the building and into the cool fall air. She zipped up her sweatshirt and flipped the hood up.

"You want to tell me what we're really outside for?"

"Patience," he said, sounding remarkably like a kindergarten teacher. They walked nearly a mile and stopped in front of a 24-hour diner, not a coffee shop. When she opened the door, the smell of bacon and last night's pot of coffee hit her.

A bored waitress lounged behind a counter lined with bar stools. She pushed herself up from her elbows and took two small plates from a metal shelf.

Kevin chose a booth in the back. "Two slices of cherry and two cups of coffee," he called to the waitress, who was already reaching into a plexiglass case.

"They must know you here," Navy said.

"Everything else here is shit, so it's empty most of the time," Kevin said. He looked up as the waitress approached. "No offense, Daisy."

She revealed a gap-toothed smile as she poured Kevin's coffee. "None taken. I only make the pies." Daisy filled Navy's cup too, then set a ceramic bowl on the table. "Cream and sugar for you." A small plastic bear filled with amber honey appeared in front of Kevin, whisked down from the tray. "Honey for you." Daisy left the pie on the edge of the table, then disappeared into the kitchen.

Navy poured in cream and watched her coffee go from black to tan. Kevin would explain himself when he was ready. Her first sip confirmed the coffee was last night's pot. She added more cream. And some sugar.

Kevin tapped his fork against the chipped white plate. "You seem relieved. You shouldn't be."

"I'm cleared. That's good, right?"

"Out of the frying pan and into the fire."

Navy cupped her hands around the mug to feel its warmth. It was the only thing the coffee was good for. "Okay, I'll bite. Why should I be worried now?"

"Oh, lots of reasons," Kevin said. "Let's start with your private key, the one you've been using to decrypt Min Gyu's messages. You need to give it to Saul."

"No. My key is signed by—"

"Yeah, web of trust and all that, I remember. You still need to give your key to Saul."

"I won't—"

"Think of the stakes here, Navy. Think of your reputation."

"Exactly." Navy set her coffee down a little too hard. "You wouldn't understand."

"What wouldn't I understand?"

"The CIA is your world. I've been here less than two years. Half my friends think I sold my soul to take this job. If it gets out that I gave away my private key, no one outside the agency would ever trust me again."

"No one has to know," Kevin said. "Let Saul use the key pair you have now. When the operation is finished, revoke the public/private key and publish a new one."

Navy's anger was blunted by her surprise. "You know a tech thing. Last year you thought encrypted firewalls existed."

"I was researching options *for you* because I knew you were going to be stubborn about this."

"Oh." Navy remembered what Kevin had said earlier. *I'm her handler.* Did Kevin still consider Navy his responsibility? "I appreciate it, but that's still not an option.

While they have my private key, they can read any encrypted messages sent to me. Not just Min Gyu's."

"Are you involved in something that would get you into trouble?" Kevin asked.

"No. And that's not the point. I don't have to be guilty to want some privacy."

"Think of the consequences here, Navy. Saul will find some judge in a secret court and get you put in jail for not cooperating. And Saul might just get the court to bankrupt you with fines on top of that."

Was Navy willing to risk all that? "I'm willing to decrypt Min Gyu's messages for as long as it takes. Isn't that enough?"

"No."

Navy wondered how long she would sit in jail before she did what Saul wanted. She honestly didn't know. But she sure as hell wasn't going to fold before Saul demonstrated how far he would go. No matter what Kevin said. "Then I'll decrypt Min Gyu's messages from a jail cell."

"Jesus Christ, Navy. Min Gyu is manipulating you using your principles. Don't you see that? You don't owe him anything."

"Should I be offended that someone thinks I have principles?" Navy fired back.

"No, you should be reading this situation better. Min Gyu wants you in the loop because he doesn't trust Saul, and he shouldn't. But Saul isn't going to let you in on all the conversations he's having with his team."

"Wait, back up. Why shouldn't he trust Saul?"

"Saul's in this for the glory. He'll screw over Min Gyu if it's convenient. And Min Gyu will hold you responsible." Kevin stuck a forkful of pie in his mouth, as if he had just delivered this week's weather report.

Navy had lost her appetite. "I don't understand. Why would Min Gyu blame me for what Saul does?"

"Min Gyu thinks he knows you. He read something about you, thinks you're like him, another persecuted soul. He thinks you'll protect him."

"You got all of that from two emails."

"It's my job to know people. I've run assets in a dozen different countries. Different conflicts, different cultures, but some things are universal. A desperate asset is tricky. Min Gyu feels betrayed. By his uncle, by his country, by us. We are not his friends. You are not his friend. He just thinks you'll keep your word. Which is dangerous for you."

Navy tried to imagine the human pieces of the puzzle as if they were a mechanical device. Gears that turned, or ground against each other. "Because if Saul betrays him, all of his anger shifts to me."

"Now you understand. Regardless of what Saul does, we need to make sure this ends in one of two ways: either Min Gyu gets here, or he dies in the process."

She sipped the bitter coffee to feel something warm inside. "You want me to be ready to kill a man in self-defense from half a world away."

"Code is a weapon. You know that better than anyone. One word from him and Office 91's next target could be you." Kevin took a bite of pie. "Now let's get back to that private key."

"Still not giving it up."

Kevin sighed. "I figured. We need to talk to your manager, Lindsey."

Navy nearly spilled her coffee. "How do you know my manager?"

Kevin dialed a number on his phone and hit the speaker button. "The Hackerville op. I was checking up on you before I agreed to let you go."

The phone continued to ring on the other end. Navy felt a mild panic. What was Kevin's plan? Events were moving too fast, and out of her control. "You don't have to help," Navy said. "I'm not asking you for any and if I'm in as much trouble as you say I am—"

"You'll throw yourself on a grenade for a goddamn stranger, but you won't accept help from a friend?" Kevin asked. "If you're going to be stubborn, the least you can do is let me try to protect you from the consequences."

While Navy was trying to process the thought that Kevin considered her a friend, Lindsey answered.

"I just had the most interesting conversation with Saul," Lindsey said. "I don't suppose that's why you're calling?"

"Did you promise him anything?" Kevin asked.

"Only that I'd talk to Navy about giving up her private key."

"Navy's right here," Kevin said. "But I wouldn't waste your breath."

"You understand, don't you?" Navy asked Lindsey.

"I mean, I understand," Lindsey said. "But do you understand the pressure you're going to be under?"

Navy sighed. "Just tell me what Saul's next move will be."

"Saul's trying to get custom malware on your work laptop. My guess is he already tried some of our basic tools. He was babbling on about virtual machines and how he couldn't reach your key file, but I don't think he really understood any of it."

"Are you saying they put a keylogger on my laptop and they already have the passphrase?" Navy felt her back stiffen. She hadn't anticipated they would go that far. She had been naïve, of course, to think the issue was settled just because she refused the first time they asked.

"I don't know, Navy," Lindsey said. "What I do know is Saul is very aware of how much it would help his career if this operation is successful."

"That's our angle," Kevin said. "Saul has a reputation for cutting other people down to get ahead. Nobody likes him."

"Not very many people like *you*," Lindsey said. Navy could hear a smile in Lindsey's voice. "How does Saul's unpopularity help us?"

"People *respect* me," Kevin said. "Even if they don't like me. Saul has history with the offensive tool group. There was a programmer Saul threw under the bus a few years ago . . . Jason? Jeff?"

"Jefferson," Lindsey said. "Jefferson volunteered to go in the field. Saul messed up and put Jefferson in a bad situation, then blamed Jefferson for not following protocol to the letter. Saul got promoted. Jefferson was demoted down to entry-level."

"Perfect," Kevin said. "We go to the offensive tools group, remind them what Saul did to the last coder that tried to help. They won't want to help Saul because they'll risk getting blamed for something they didn't do. And we'll stress that since Navy is willing to decrypt Min Gyu's messages, nothing will be delayed if the offensive tools group just . . . deprioritizes giving Saul what he wants."

"And if they delay long enough, hopefully it won't matter anyway," Lindsey said. "It might work."

Navy thought the whole thing sounded convoluted. How could Kevin be so certain everyone would react as he expected? But she certainly didn't have a better plan. "I should say thank you," Navy said. "And I am grateful. I just . . ." *I don't want anyone else to suffer for my decision.*

"Navy," Lindsey said. "You are one of my best analysts. We are buried under work right now. If it makes you feel better, think of this less as a personal favor and more as me protecting my own ass."

"I'm not sure I can buy enough *World's Best Boss* mugs to pay you back," Navy said. "But thank you."

"You can pay me back by not changing your passphrase until this is all over," Lindsey said. "You're not supposed to know Saul might have it."

Fuck. But Navy knew Lindsey was right. "So I'm compromising my principles either way."

"You seem to have a knack for finding interesting situations," Lindsey said. "Be glad you have Kevin on your side this time."

"I'll be back in the office soon," Kevin said. "I'll come to you."

After Kevin hung up, he gathered his things and waited for Navy.

"I think I need a minute," Navy said. "I'll follow in a bit."

"Does this mean you might change your mind?" Kevin asked.

"No." Navy chewed on her lip. "This political play you're making to get the offensive tools group to stall, what are the odds of it working?"

"Fifty-fifty."

"Why is it you never give me good news?"

He grinned. "You should at least sample the pie. Daisy makes the best pie on the Eastern seaboard."

Chapter 8

Kevin took the bus to Irving's neighborhood. He walked past crumbling brownstones and an elementary school, closed since the seventies. Behind the splintered plywood covering the windows, he heard the clank of an empty can. Spray paint, perhaps, or the breakfast beer of one of the homeless people who lived inside. More like brunch, he supposed. Traveling for work often left him jetlagged, and Kevin slept in on weekends out of habit.

Last year, Jackson had challenged Kevin "to do something a good person might do" and Kevin joined the Big Brother program. Kevin chose Irving as his little brother after checking out the family thoroughly. Fighting uphill battles he could do. Lost causes weren't his thing.

Irving's father, a staff sergeant in the army, had died in Afghanistan several years ago. Mom worked two jobs and did her best to keep the family finances above water. Irving was a teenager who loved video games and perhaps was motivated by his mother's struggles, read every book he could find on monetary policy and personal finance. If Irving's family had more money, he would be on the fast track to a four-year degree and a lucrative position on Wall Street.

But in this universe, Irving was just a good kid who, with a little bit of luck, might survive this neighborhood. Kevin hated relying on luck. On Kevin's first forays into the neighborhood, he didn't come to see Irving. He approached the problem as he would any assignment. Go in undercover as someone forgettable, someone homeless perhaps. Then once you identify the threats to your mission, neutralize them. Kevin had known exactly how his confrontations with dangerous characters in Irving's neighborhood would go, which was exactly how it went. Despots and street thugs weren't so different. Mostly male, mostly violent, and always greedy for power.

Kevin made sure his opponents understood that it was by his choice they walked away. He had explained that he was not after their territory or their business. He had informed them, in detail, of everything he knew about their affairs. Nothing would change, he had assured them, as long as he and Irving and Irving's mother were left alone. He knew that one apex predator would recognize another, and he would make with them the same deal predators had been making with each other for thousands of years: mutual avoidance.

The modest brick apartment building where Irving lived was no better, or worse, than the rest of the block. Kevin had never been inside, but he knew what he would find. Lead paint and carpet well beyond its useful life. Kevin rapped on the door twice and waited. Five minutes later footsteps clattered down a set of stairs. Irving wore a black shirt printed with the profile of his favorite football star, baggy jean shorts, and sneakers whose soles flapped against the linoleum.

Irving carefully held the door so Kevin couldn't see inside. "My mom would come down," he said. "But she's sleeping."

Kevin didn't work multiple shifts but he knew from timezone hopping how hard it was to find enough hours to sleep in a day. "Sure," he said. "I understand."

Irving nodded uncertainly, then shut the door behind him.

He's not an asset, Kevin reminded himself. He pulled his hands out of his pocket and tried for a genuine smile that stretched unfamiliar muscles. "Your mom works hard."

Then, wondering if he had sounded condescending, he cleared his throat. "She works at the grocery store, right?"

The boy eyed him cautiously. "Yeah. And the gas station."

Kevin wondered again why he had taken up Jackson's challenge to be a big brother. Being nice, caring, and compassionate weren't his strong points. "I thought we might go to Kicks today. I could buy you some new shoes."

Irving's angry sneer caught Kevin off guard. "My mom and I don't need charity."

There went Kevin's plan for the day. Most people were happy to receive gifts. No, Kevin corrected himself, assets were always happy to receive gifts. They were always asking for favors, even before he'd offered. Irving was just a teenager with an ego and pride, like all teenagers.

"Fuck it," Irving said. "I told Mom this was a bad idea when she signed me up."

"Watch your language," Kevin heard himself say. The paternal instinct surprised him. "I mean, I'm sorry. I didn't mean anything by it. I just got this bonus at work, and I thought—" No words came to mind that would answer Irving's accusation. "We could just do ice cream again." Like they did every week. The sullen cashier at Burger King would take his order for two ice cream sundaes, then give them two mounds of soft serve that looked nothing like the pictures on the menu. Then he and Irving would sit in silence until the remains of their sundaes melted.

"That'd be okay."

They started walking on the scarred sidewalk, Kevin's long, spindly legs and the boy's shorter ones somehow in sync. With each step, the worn-out shoes slapped the sidewalk.

"Goodwill, maybe," Irving said.

"For ice cream?"

"Shoes. That way Mom won't ask."

Kevin nodded. "Goodwill it is."

Irving stared down at his shoes as they walked. As they passed a tall building, the sun caught Irving's profile, and Kevin noticed a slight purple swelling around the kid's left eye. Suddenly, Kevin understood why Irving was reluctant to be seen in new shoes.

"What happened to your eye?"

The boy's sloped back went straight. "Nothing."

Finally, a problem Kevin knew how to deal with. "I can help. I know a few things."

"A white boy like you?" Irving's eyes were scornful as he noted Kevin's button-down shirt and business-casual slacks. "Sure you do. Like how to set up a 401(k). Or hire a personal trainer."

Kevin eyed an empty soccer field with goals missing nets. "How about we cover those lessons next week? I'll make you a deal. You tell me who beat you up, and I'll teach you a few moves."

"We can still get shoes?"

"We can still get shoes."

Irving glanced around the empty street. "It's this kid at school, Tony. And his friends. Last week they took my wallet. This week they searched me and emptied my pockets. Every time they beat me up, it's a little worse."

Tony might be a future delinquent, but the name wasn't familiar to Kevin. He hid his sigh of relief. No drug dealers to take down. Just some bullies. He veered left, toward the empty field, and Irving followed.

"First thing you need to do is find all the cameras at your school. Make sure Tony attacks you where it can be recorded."

"I'm no snitch. I don't want to report him. I want him to leave me alone."

Kevin leaned down until he was at Irving's level. "If you want Tony to leave you alone, you're going to have to hurt him. And if you hurt him, you may get in trouble."

Irving didn't look satisfied.

"And if you get in trouble, it has to be clear who started it."

"Oh," Irving said.

"Always think strategically." Kevin straightened. "Now, pretend you're Tony and I'm you. Show me how he attacks."

Chapter 9

Jackson really wanted working air conditioning. The refugee center's counseling rooms had no windows and the vents spit out warm air, even in the summer. He also really wanted a pen. But this patient wouldn't allow Jackson to take notes. Like all his patients, Dahlia had no idea he was a CIA field agent. He forgave himself for the deception. To protect the center, he used an alias. And nothing he heard during counseling sessions ever made its way into a CIA file, despite Kevin's insistence.

If Kevin knew what Jackson's patients talked about, he'd stop asking.

Dahlia had survived the genocide in Rwanda as a teenager. She had been raped and left for dead. She spent the next nine months pregnant in a refugee camp. The baby she hadn't wanted died soon after birth. These were the things Jackson expected she might want to discuss.

Instead, she was talking about *him* again.

"My roommate knew we were dating. And then I go away on a trip, I come back, and I find them on the couch together."

"I can see why that would upset you. Did you two ever talk about it?"

"I confronted her, like you said, and ..."

Jackson had suggested Dahlia calmly tell her roommate how she felt. He kept his face neutral while he waited for Dahlia to finish her thought.

"We ended up at each other's throats. Our neighbors called the cops."

"What did she say that made you so angry?" Given her circumstances, it wasn't surprising Dahlia was struggling. Surviving trauma left scars. But in the year since he'd started therapy sessions with Dahlia, her story hadn't changed. Every session it was about a guy she had lost.

"She said it was my fault because I was terrible in bed. She said—" Dahlia looked at the box of tissues on the table, then cleared her throat.

"This is a safe place," Jackson told her. If she would let herself feel something other than anger, she might move forward. He wondered if it was time to push a little harder. He handed her the box of tissues. "Tell me what she said."

Her tears erupted into a fistful of white tissues. "That I didn't move." Each word was marked by a sob. "That all I would do is just lay there."

Jackson could tell by the fear in her eyes that she knew why she couldn't move during sex, and she knew why the comment had triggered such rage.

"All of my friends have families, or at least boyfriends." She sniffed back another sob. "I want that. I want kids. Before it's too late."

The clock on the wall said her session was over, but this was his last session of the day. The room would be free for a while longer. "Were you ever close to your roommate?"

"When we first moved in together, I guess."

"So you two hung out? Talked?"

She smiled, the first time he'd ever seen her smile. "We had fun. We went dancing a lot."

It was a common pattern for those afraid of intimacy, arranging social contact that provided the illusion of connection. "Anything else?" Jackson felt sweat gathering behind his knees in the warm room. By the time he got home, he'd smell like he'd been to the gym.

"I guess not." She twisted used tissues between her fingers. "Do you think ... do you think that means something?"

For Dahlia, this was a breakthrough. The first hint of awareness in how her past had put her present into a loop. "I know we've talked about this before, and you rejected the idea, but the rape recovery group still meets on Wednesday nights at the church next door. I think you could benefit from talking with people who understand what you've been through."

She shook her head slightly. "I'm not like them."

"You've never been to a meeting. How do you know?"

"I don't cry." She threw the tissues on the floor to get rid of the evidence. "I mean, I don't normally. Even during ... even then, I didn't cry."

Navy would hate him for thinking it, but Dahlia reminded him a little of her. Both were strong in many ways and brittle in others. Women who had learned that showing emotion was a weakness. The idea was as persistent as it was wrong. "Before you started seeing me, you briefly saw two other counselors here, right?"

Her eyes were guarded. "Yes."

Jackson would have to be careful not to undo all the progress they'd made so far. "They were both women. Women who are open about their experiences as rape victims. Therapy-wise, they should have been a better fit for you. But you decided to switch. Twice. And now you've been seeing me for a year."

Dahlia stared at the picture on the wall. It was a generic shot of beaches and palm trees. Supposedly calming.

Could he push just a little harder? "I think you stopped seeing them because their experiences were too close to yours. But you knew you needed help, so you wouldn't walk away from counseling entirely."

She shifted uncomfortably on the worn couch. "So you don't want to see me anymore."

"That's not what I'm getting at. What I mean is, I think you're ready, if you want, to process what happened."

She sniffed again and picked up her purse. "We're over our time. I have to go."

Jackson wouldn't know the results of his efforts until their next appointment, nearly a month away. "See you in a few weeks."

His phone buzzed in his pocket. Just seeing Navy's name on the screen drained some of the tension from his shoulders. He leaned back in his chair and closed his eyes before answering. "Hey."

"Just wanted to tell you I'll be late for dinner. There's a new message, and I have to play middleman again." Navy sounded tired. She often worked long hours, but being on call for Saul and his team had taken its toll on her.

"How about I bring dinner to you? I was going to be late anyway."

"Appointment ran long?" Navy asked.

"For good reason."

"I look forward to hearing about your day after I finish the ritual flogging with Saul's team."

"You know, calling your meetings with Saul ritual flogging probably isn't helping your stress level."

"Aren't you supposed to be off the clock now?"

He smiled at the reminder of how lucky he was. When he met Navy, he had nearly given up on the idea of finding a partner willing to put up with his job. "Chinese or Thai food?"

"Drunken noodles, extra peanuts. And kombucha. I'm working in the conference room."

Half an hour later he was at the office bearing a plastic bag full of warm takeout boxes. He found Navy in the conference room. A sloppy ponytail left wisps of her blond hair to frame her profile. Her hands moved deftly over the keyboard, so fast he could barely follow. She was at her most graceful when she thought no one was watching.

He enjoyed the view for a second longer, then twisted the bag hanging at his side. The crinkle of the plastic startled her. Her smile was his reward.

"You're a lifesaver." She went straight for the bag of food. "I'm starving."

"Not even a kiss first?" he asked, holding the food out of her reach.

She pecked him on the cheek, then stole the food and sat down. The silence was punctuated by the click of chopsticks and slurping of noodles. Kevin would have called this stage in a relationship boring. Jackson was grateful that he and Navy were comfortable enough with each other to relax a little. Their "boring" intimacy was hard-won.

"Well, look at the two lovebirds." Kevin said as he entered the room.

"You're never going to get tired of that, are you?" Jackson asked. Jackson knew Kevin took credit for Jackson's recent closeness with Navy.

"I feel like maybe I should go into relationship counseling," Kevin said. "I'm pretty good at it."

"Gloating is generally considered unprofessional," Navy said. "How is Saul's mood today?"

"Pissed," Kevin said. "Which means I think your private key is still safe. And he's tired of Min Gyu dragging out negotiations." Kevin stole an egg roll from Jackson's meal. "Frankly, so am I. We've given Min Gyu everything he wants. I think Min Gyu's trying to decide what he can ask for to prove he should trust us."

"I wish we could fast-forward to the part where Saul takes credit for saving the world and I never have to see Peter again," Navy said.

Jackson rubbed her hand. "It's been that bad, huh?"

"Peter finds a new way to call me a traitor every time I see him."

"Some people get counseling, some people work out their issues on their coworkers," Jackson said.

Kevin laughed then checked his watch. "Game faces on. Saul and company will be here in two minutes."

"How do you *do* that?" Navy asked. "It's a little creepy you're so good at knowing exactly when they'll get here."

"Saul's coffee routine," Kevin said. "It takes him exactly five minutes to prepare his coffee just the way he wants it, and I passed by him three minutes ago."

Exactly when Kevin had predicted, four people entered the conference room. Jackson recognized the faces from the first contentious meeting: Uri, Eli, Peter, and Saul.

Saul's eyes skipped over Jackson and went straight to Navy. "I just sent the message to you. Decrypt it and we'll get out of your hair."

Navy wiped sauce off her chin and took a swig of kombucha. "Sure." Her attention swung back to her laptop. Only she and Jackson could see the screen. She typed in a long password that showed up as asterisks, then a message appeared in her terminal.

Jackson saw his own name. By the microscopic pause of Navy's hands, he knew she had seen it too.

```
Time and date agreed. Meet me inside the
abandoned steel factory just outside of
Onchon. Send Jackson to pick me up. I
won't go if he's not there.
```

"This message is corrupted," Navy said. "It won't decrypt. I'll work on it tonight." She reached up to close her screen just as Kevin caught Jackson's eye.

Kevin stole the laptop from beneath her fingers. Jackson had to put a hand on Navy's shoulder to keep her from grabbing it back.

"Min Gyu wants Jackson to retrieve him," Kevin said.

"Not an option," Navy said, alternating her glare between Kevin and Jackson.

Saul looked confused. "That's not Jackson's part of the world. And how does he even know you're together?"

"The payroll database," Navy said dully. "We have the same address." Navy understood now why Kevin had warned her about Min Gyu's state of mind. "He's testing me. Min Gyu wants someone I care about to be at risk."

"This is actually a good sign," Uri said.

"How the fuck is this a good sign?" Navy spat.

Uri spoke tentatively. "Aside from being an American agent, Jackson's no good to the North Koreans. Min Gyu is trying to show us he's not setting a trap."

"Or it's a false signal," Eli said. "To throw us off."

"You think the North Koreans would go to all this trouble to kidnap one American agent who doesn't even know our intelligence apparatus there?" Saul asked. "That doesn't make any sense."

"In the seventies, Kim Jong Il kidnapped a South Korean director because he liked his movies," Eli said. "Don't put anything past them."

"He's not going," Navy said.

Jackson's surprise was echoed by everyone in the room. Navy was headstrong, but surely she knew this wasn't her decision. "Navy—"

"I never wanted to be a part of this," Navy said. "Remember? He chose me. He only speaks through me. And I won't send the message saying you're coming."

Jackson nudged a takeout box out of the way to touch her hand. "There's a good chance this is real. I have to go."

Navy shook her head. "I won't do it. This isn't your risk to take."

"Look at that," Peter sneered. "The traitor has morals."

It was only Jackson's arm that kept Navy on her side of the table. The outburst wouldn't help her reputation.

Peter kept going. "It's exactly what she did before. She thinks she knows what's right, and she's not going to listen to anyone else. Even if it puts other people at risk."

"That's enough," Saul said. "I think we all know what has to happen. Kevin, you're her handler. Handle her."

The team left. Kevin stayed with Jackson and Navy. For the second time that day, Jackson was staring at a woman with wet eyes. Navy got up and paced the room. Jackson should know what to say. It was his job to always know what to say. Part of him was flattered by her open affection for him. Part of him was angry that it would make doing what he had to do harder.

Navy came to a stop in front of Kevin. "You know this is a bad idea."

Jackson started to answer, but Kevin spoke first. "He has to go, Navy. Min Gyu is testing you *and* he's trying to prove it's not a setup. Jackson has to go." Kevin stood up and gently pressed down on Navy's shoulders until she was sitting. "And you have to send that message."

Navy spun her chair toward Jackson. Her hazel eyes glittered with unshed tears. "Is that what you want me to do?"

Jackson swallowed over the painful lump in his throat. "We don't have a choice."

"That's not what you said when I went to Romania last year."

"That was different."

Kevin nailed Jackson with a disapproving glare.

"Okay, it wasn't that different," Jackson said. "You had to go to Romania. I have to do this."

Navy's breath came out of her nostrils in bursts. She put herself between Kevin and Jackson.

"I'm holding you responsible for whatever happens, Kevin," Navy said. "Make sure Saul treats Min Gyu well, and Jackson comes back alive."

Kevin's somber face showed a newfound respect for her. "That's fair."

"Now that I've been *handled*, may I leave?" But she didn't wait for Kevin's permission. In one motion she grabbed her laptop and slammed it shut. She swung her bag over her shoulder and stormed out the door Saul had left open.

Navy's half-eaten dinner was cold and shiny with oil. The smell of peanuts made the room seem claustrophobic. Undaunted, Kevin grabbed a fresh pair of chopsticks and Navy's takeout box. "What's wrong with her?" he asked. "She's normally smarter than this."

Jackson's anger found a new target, even though he knew the mess wasn't Kevin's fault. Not entirely, anyway. "It's too familiar. She still holds herself responsible for Sara's rape and Moss' kidnapping."

"Because she happened to be born with a resemblance to Erin?" Kevin slurped a mouthful of noodles. "That's ridiculous."

"Not everyone is the paragon of humanity you are."

Kevin's chopsticks clicked twice. "You're angry that I called Navy out in front of Saul just now."

"You didn't have to embarrass her. We could have dealt with it privately."

"No, I had to. To protect her." Kevin raised his eyebrows, his only recognition of Jackson's glare. "Saul has double-checked everything Navy's told him. Even I could smell bullshit in her explanation. Saul has to think I'm on his side, or I'll be out of the loop. And that would make it harder to protect Navy."

Jackson threw his own half-eaten food in the small garbage can by the wall. "If you say so."

"How long have we worked together?"

"Longer than I care to remember."

"And I've always protected you."

It was true, as much as Jackson hated to admit it.

"Everything I'm doing is to protect you and Navy. You'll just have to trust me."

"Yeah, well, fuck you very much." He was two strides outside the door when Kevin spoke again.

"If you need a place to sleep tonight, let me know. I've slept on your couch. It's terrible."

Jackson went to find Navy. He tried her phone first, unsurprised when she didn't answer. She wasn't at home. Or at any of their usual restaurants and bars. Next stop: her gym. She had just switched to a larger one for its 24-hour workout room stocked with punching bags. He was relieved to find her car in the crowded lot but hesitated before getting out of his own.

Jackson had been so preoccupied with finding her, he hadn't considered what he would say. He doubted she would be happy to see him. With a click, Jackson turned the car lights off. In front of him, traffic whizzed by on the turnpike, red in one direction, yellow in the other. Hundreds of people, living normal lives, passing him right by. Jackson could be one of them. Give up the game. Worst-case scenario for this operation was he left Navy alone and his family with some bullshit story about why his body couldn't be found. Best-case scenario was winning a medal Jackson couldn't tell anyone about.

Never mind the right words. Navy needed to know Jackson was there. That was the important part.

The chilled air of the gym was a relief after the humid evening. The coolness didn't stop people from sweating. Grunts from the last boxing class of the day echoed off the cinderblock walls. No one was sitting at the check-in desk.

Jackson walked past it toward the sound of fists hitting leather. The heavy bag, marked with the outline of a human being, was taking a beating. Navy was faster than he remembered, but it had been a while since he'd seen her fight. She glanced at him, then tightened her lips and nailed the bag with a roundhouse kick. Better than a knee to the groin, he supposed.

It was nearly 9:00 and the room was empty except for them.

"We should talk," Jackson said.

Navy flattened a hand and made a well-aimed chop to the neck of the human outline. "So talk."

"I understand why—"

Navy whirled toward Jackson. "Of course you fucking understand. It's your job. You're going to tell me I shouldn't feel guilty about what happened two and a half years ago because it wasn't my fault."

That about covered it. "Then maybe we can move on to why *I'm* upset."

Confusion creased her face. She steadied the bag as it brushed her forehead. "I was the one who got humiliated in front of everyone. What do you have to be upset about?"

Kevin could have handled the situation in the conference room better, but that wasn't the only thing bothering Jackson. "My job is part of who I am. I defend other people by putting myself in harm's way."

"This is d—"

"And, yes, this is different," Jackson said. "This is more dangerous than what I usually do. It's not how I usually get my assignments. But the principle is the same." He glanced around to make sure they were still alone. "If this operation is successful, thousands of people will be safer for it."

"As if I don't know that," Navy shot back.

81

"I don't need you making me feel guilty for wanting to do my job."

"Do you really mean that?" Navy's anger sharpened her words to a point; Jackson felt each one as a stab in his gut. "Would you rather I not care?"

Goddamit. He was doing it again. The same fight that had ended the handful of relationships before Navy. "No, I don't mean . . . I'm sorry."

His previous girlfriends had never known what he really did. But they knew the important things. *You go to dangerous places. You're out of contact for weeks at a time, I never know when you're coming home. What should I feel exactly?*

"I guess I'm feeling guilty," Jackson said. "I know why you're worried. I don't like hurting you. But this is my job. It's the work I want to do. I know it's hard to understand—"

"Of course I understand." The words were curt instead of angry. "Remember when I went underground? And you wanted to go with me? I know it hurt you when I went alone. But that's the work I had to do."

Jackson risked stepping closer to Navy. She didn't move away.

"Aren't we a pair?" he said.

"Always hurting each other," she said.

"For the right reasons?" Jackson wondered aloud.

"Just because I understand why you have to go doesn't mean I can be graceful about it." Navy shook her head. At Jackson or at the situation, he couldn't say.

"We've worked so hard to get where we are," Navy said. She laced her hands through his. "I've never been as close with anyone as I've been with you."

"Me either." The past six months had been intense. Dealing with her past had enabled them to find an emotional intimacy whose depth surprised him.

Jackson had to prepare her for the worst. "You're strong. I want you to be happy. If I don't come back—"

"Don't." Her hands clenched painfully around his. "Just don't."

Jackson kissed her forehead, still salty with sweat. "I'm sorry. You're right." But she knew what he had been about to say, and that was the important part.

Chapter 10

For the first time, Kevin was looking forward to his volunteer gig as a big brother. Irving had picked up quickly on the Krav Maga moves they'd practiced last week. Kevin had even seen Irving smile. Helping Irving with his bully problem would be a welcome distraction from last week's disastrous meeting with Navy. She still wasn't talking to him.

He skipped up the sagging steps of Irving's brownstone. Irving opened the door before Kevin even knocked. Irving held a finger to his lips to tell Kevin to be quiet. Kevin was more focused on the teenager's two black eyes.

"I don't want to wake up Mom," Irving whispered as he gently closed the door.

Not wanting to wake his mother up was nothing new, but the whispers and theatrics were.

"I pretended to be asleep last night when she came home from her shift," Irving said once they were clear of the house. "So she fell asleep in the living room. She does that when she wants to catch me before I go out."

Kevin's attempts to help the boy had only led to more injury, and now he was an accessory to sneaking Irving out of the house. "She should know you're hurt," Kevin said.

Irving shook his head so emphatically it looked painful. "It will look better tomorrow. I can avoid her until then."

Guilt was an unfamiliar emotion for Kevin. "You can tell her it's my fault."

"No." A mixture of defiance and fear swirled in the boy's dark eyes. "It's Tony's fault. Him and his friends. I didn't do anything to them. I just want them to leave me alone."

Kevin had seen that look before. The best fighters weren't motivated by bloodlust, but conviction. Conviction, however, should always be tempered with reality. "Look, if they're not going to back down, you're just going to get hurt more."

"I fought them off the first time," Irving said proudly. "Three of them. I just need a little more training."

The humidity of the day seeped into Kevin's armpits. "And what happened the second time?"

A dandelion had found its way through the cracked concrete. The globe of fragile seeds vibrated in the wind. Irving kicked at the bloom; the seeds floated through the chain-link fence, over the soccer field and its patches of brown grass. "They had a knife. You can get me a knife, right?"

Kevin suppressed a bitter smile. Yeah, he could get Irving a knife. He might even be able to teach Irving how to handle it. Kevin also knew giving Irving a weapon was a terrible idea. "What's the most important thing I taught you about fighting?"

"To think strategically."

"And what do you think will happen if you're caught with a knife?"

Irving kicked the dandelion again. "I'll say I had it for self-defense."

"You going to bet your future on that excuse working?"

"I seen people get away with plenty," Irving spat back.

Kevin shoved his hands into his pockets and felt the knife he kept there. "They're not really getting away with it. Their record—even their juvenile record—will follow them. Five years from now the only job they'll be able to get is pushing a broom in the jail they'll end up in."

Irving's combative posture told Kevin he wasn't convinced.

"This isn't just about you. How do you think your mom would feel?"

Kevin anticipated the punch. He deflected Irving's arm and stepped back. This was a critical point in the process of earning Irving's loyalty. Push him too hard and Kevin would lose him. Don't push him enough and the boy would make a mistake he couldn't recover from. "You know the system's not fair. Two miles from here there's a rich prep school where white boys wear uniforms and smoke pot in the bathrooms, maybe even snort a little powder. When they get caught, their parents schmooze with the principal or hire an expensive lawyer, and the whole thing goes away. You don't get to make the same mistakes. Your landing won't be so soft." He put a hand on the boy's shoulder. Irving didn't flinch, a good sign. "I want to help you. I will help you. But you can't afford to make stupid mistakes. You have to listen to me."

"So what do we do?" Irving asked.

"We start with the principal."

Irving groaned. "You said you were going to help. The principal won't do anything."

"Exactly. Think."

Beyond the rows of dilapidated brownstones, Kevin could see a gleaming condominium high-rise next to a swanky hotel. A few miles, but it might as well have been another universe. The chain-link fence rattled as Irving leaned against it. "It's a trail. Like the cameras. So when they get hurt, I can prove it's self-defense," Irving said.

The "when" rather than an "if" was a nice touch, Kevin thought. "Good. You make a report. It'll get buried. We can work with that."

"And then what? I just let them beat me up?"

"For a little bit." Irving's bullies were escalating. If Kevin let things take their natural course, until it was bad enough for the school to intervene, it wouldn't end well for Irving. "Just because your opponent has a weapon doesn't mean you have to lose. But these moves take practice. So we'll have to see each other more often. And you don't use them until I say you're ready."

Irving's eyes lit up. "You mean I won't get cut?"

Some things could not be said gently. "No, you'll get cut. But you can still win." Kevin picked up a discarded magazine, blown against the fence by a strong wind. Last night's rain had crackled and stiffened the pages. When rolled up, the paper had a satisfying weight and a blunt end. It would work.

Now they just needed a location with a little more privacy. Kevin crossed the soccer field and Irving followed. Behind a storage shed, there was a small patch of dirt that backed up to an alley behind a bar. Good. It wouldn't be open for a few hours.

Despite his earlier bravado, Irving looked nervous and unsteady. Training would make him steady. For Irving's sake, Kevin hoped the nerves would never go away.

"The key to a knife defense is specificity and tenaciousness," Kevin said. "You will get cut. But if you counter with the right attack, you can get away." He sorted through the knife approaches in his head and picked the one most used by muggers and punks. He held the rolled-up magazine in his right hand near Irving's waist, and with a bent elbow. "He started like this, right? He's right-handed?"

Irving nodded.

"To survive a knife attack you must do three things nearly simultaneously: push, grab, hit. Push the knife away, grab the arm for control, and hit to prevent your attacker from recovering."

Irving bit his lip before nodding.

"First, push my arm across my body and step a little to the side."

The push wasn't nearly strong enough.

"Don't worry about hurting me. Slap my hand as hard as you can."

Irving set his jaw, then swung wide before connecting with Kevin's hand. The back of Kevin's hand stung. Better. Kevin held his arm where Irving's blow had sent it.

"Now take your left arm and grab just behind my wrist on the inside, push your elbow against my shoulder. Use your right hand to grab my wrist."

"Like this?" Irving's grip was surprisingly strong.

Kevin suppressed a grin. "Yeah, like that. That's the push and the grab." The real finishing move for this sequence was to sweep your attacker's hand to his own neck and cut his throat. That was probably too much. "Now pull my arm back and use your left hand to strike at my neck with the edge of your palm."

Irving was still too tentative.

"Let's go from the beginning," Kevin said, holding out the magazine. "I attack and you—" Kevin's hand was slapped aside, then Irving's strong fingers dug into the tender skin at Kevin's wrist. Irving's open palm brushed his neck.

"Again," Kevin said. "Push, grab, hit." Kevin held out the magazine and Irving repeated the maneuver. But this time, Kevin dodged the blow to his neck. "The hit can be anything. A kick to the groin, stomping on their foot, a kick at the knee, whatever you can reach. Keep hitting until they drop the knife."

They practiced until Kevin's dress shirt was damp with sweat. "That's enough for today. You did well." He rested a hand on the boy's shoulder. Irving's shirt was moist too. "But you're not ready yet. There are other attacks we need to cover."

"Tomorrow night," Irving said. "Can we practice tomorrow night?"

Kevin thought about his empty social calendar. "That'll work. Stay safe."

He whistled softly on his way to the bus stop. At least he had done one good deed for the day. And the mock fight had drained some of his tension about Jackson being sent to retrieve Min Gyu. If Navy hadn't lost her temper in front of Saul, Kevin might have told her that he was just as unhappy about Min Gyu asking for Jackson. Kevin would be sending Jackson into a completely unfamiliar hostile environment. Drop Jackson off in the middle of Afghanistan, and he would likely pop up a week later just fine. If something went wrong on the pickup in North Korea, Kevin wasn't sure the result would be the same.

"I saw your impromptu fighting lesson. I didn't figure you for someone who did charity work. Is your little brother trying to get out of a gang or into one?"

The man who stepped out from the alley next to the bus stop was the last person Kevin expected to see. "Saul." He left Saul's question unanswered.

"Navy sent the final details on Min Gyu's pickup yesterday. Jackson ships out in five days."

Kevin knew all this. "Is there a reason we're talking here instead of at the office?"

"I haven't decided about you yet."

"Decided about what exactly?"

"Whether you're working with me or against me."

"I'm working for the operation."

Saul's lips flicked into a tight smile. "You're very good at dodging questions. I suppose that's necessary for you. I prefer to work more directly."

"Let me be direct then." Kevin could see his bus approaching. He figured he had one minute. Then there would be witnesses. "You're looking for a way to capture your prize without dealing with the troublesome details of resettling a possibly hostile North Korean defector. You're thinking maybe you pick up Min Gyu, make a pit stop on the way back, and force Min Gyu's cooperation without giving him a life here."

"Is that a problem? That's the best thing for everyone."

"You're underestimating Min Gyu. You're assuming he only has one signal he can send."

Saul looked confused.

The bus was two blocks away now. "You don't survive as long as he has without learning to make a few moral sacrifices. Min Gyu was in our payroll database. He figured out Navy and Jackson were living together. Min Gyu could easily be building dossiers on other employees. Including you. I guarantee he has a backup plan, if you don't treat him well. Maybe he'll sell the data he found to the highest bidder. Maybe he'll use the data to expose our agents. But whatever it is, you should be concerned."

The crease on Saul's forehead told Kevin he'd hit his mark.

"The *best thing for everyone* is if Min Gyu arrives on U.S. soil alive and well," Kevin said. "If Jackson or Navy is harmed because you dropped the ball, I'll see to it your career at the agency is over."

A screech of brakes announced there was only one stop sign before the conversation ended. "I have friends in the agency, too," Saul said.

"Yeah, but you don't have Navy. If she decides to hurt you, you'll never see it coming."

Chapter 11

Erin weighed the sealed shoe box in one hand, then studied Jackson's profile against a blue sky dotted with clouds. The weather was perfect, rare in DC, and they had decided to meet at the park next to Erin's apartment.

"This is a bit morbid, don't you think?" she asked.

"Just promise me you'll deliver it to Navy ... in case."

Erin pressed the neatly folded brown paper at the corners, considering what items might be inside. Sentimental knickknacks? A sappy letter? More than that, surely. The box was heavy.

Nearby, a family was having a picnic in the grass. The two kids ran around adding grass stains to their designer jeans. The dad rested on a picnic blanket with the coat for his suit carefully folded and set to the side. Did they know, Erin wondered, what people like her risked for them? Did they know the people who took those risks always left someone behind?

"Oh, that depends," Erin said. "You're planning on coming back, right?"

"Of course I'm planning on coming back."

"You've never given me a 'just in case' package before."

"I'll be crawling through makeshift tunnels under a demilitarized zone into unfamiliar, hostile territory to meet someone who may or may not arrange for me to spend the rest of my life in a North Korean prison camp. A little caution seems warranted."

"Sounds like an interesting weekend."

"Then maybe you should go," he snapped.

"You know I would take your place."

Jackson sighed and planted his elbows on his knees. "Yeah, I know."

"We'll take care of her, I promise." Erin pressed the package into her lap, felt the corners dig in. "But I think you'll be fine. Can't be any worse than making arms deals with Afghani warlords."

"I know people in Afghanistan. I speak Pashto and some Dari. There's no room for mistakes here, Erin." The fatigue evident in his eyes roughened his voice. "If this goes sideways, I won't make it out."

She had never seen him this worried about an operation before. But he wasn't wrong. A good person would make up some sort of reassuring lie. The trouble was, Erin wasn't a good person. "Navy understands why you're going, whatever she says."

"I learned this week how they teach math in North Korea." Jackson rubbed his forehead with both hands, then slid his fingers down to his neck. "You have killed one American soldier. You kill two more. How many soldiers have you killed total? In kindergarten, children play a game where they attack hook-nosed American dummies with toy guns and batons."

A light breeze stirred the grass. Erin thought about what the weather would be like on the other side of the world. She should go. She and Jackson had the same title. But she thrived on risk. Jackson only tolerated it. Erin was known for doing operations no one else would do. Operations that required a certain level of ruthlessness most agents didn't possess. Screw the box. Anyone could deliver a box.

"I'll take care of this," she said.

"Thanks."

After Jackson left, Erin pulled out her cell phone. Kevin didn't answer on the first ring, or the second. On the third, he answered panting.

"In the middle of training," he said.

In the background, she heard a muffled higher pitched voice. A young boy's, maybe. "Four days until Jackson leaves, right?"

"Yeah?"

"You're going with him?"

"On this one? Of course. I don't trust Saul."

"I want to be on Jackson's insertion team."

The panting stopped. "Your handler won't be happy with me."

"You know Jackson could use the help. He's too good for his own good."

"Yeah, we could use you."

"Then I'm in. Do me a favor, and let's keep this a surprise."

Kevin laughed. "Sure, why not. Jackson's already furious with me."

Chapter 12

Navy woke early and knew exactly why. Jackson was out of bed. She didn't bother to reach for her phone to check the time. Judging by the pitch-black outside and Jackson's absence, she knew it was after four a.m. but not before five. If she turned to face the closet, she would see closed doors rimmed with light. Like in her very own horror movie.

Horror movie wasn't too far off, actually. Behind the closet doors, Navy knew Jackson was packing the last few items in his bag. When he walked out the front door, he would be walking toward the most dangerous mission he had ever been on. And it was all Navy's fault. Three years ago, she had decided not to die quietly like she was supposed to. For a few short months, she had been famous or infamous, depending on who you asked. And now, half a world away, a man had decided to use Navy as his ticket out.

Navy didn't know if Min Gyu deserved to be saved. She didn't know if Min Gyu could dismantle North Korea's nuclear weapons program. All Navy knew was right now she felt like she was drowning. If Jackson died, it would be her fault. Just like Sara and Moss almost dying had been her fault. All because of her face.

Her stupid fucking face.

Navy heard the only zipper in the house she knew by sound. The sound meant Jackson had just finished packing the small canvas bag he took on most of his operations.

Would he come over to wake her? He always did. Except that one time. When he had been angry at her the morning he left.

Navy heard the light click off inside the closet. Then, quietly, gently, the doors opened and Jackson padded across the room. Then the sounds of the coffee maker from the kitchen.

Navy lay in bed, waiting. Staring at the wall. Was now really the time to be stubborn? If Jackson didn't come back, she would regret—Navy cut off the thought. Jackson would come back. The alternative was too hard to contemplate.

So go to him.

But she didn't move. The coffee machine finished. Cabinets opened and closed. Navy could see Jackson's face clearly in her mind and had no idea what she would say to him.

A triangle of light speared the room as Jackson opened the bedroom door. Navy smelled something sweet and burnt from the kitchen—cinnamon?

"Navy?" Jackson walked over to her side of the bed. He saw her wide-open eyes and seemed relieved. "You're awake."

She sat up and felt cold as the sheets fell away. "Of course I am." Then realizing how she must have sounded, "I mean, I didn't want to miss . . ." *Saying goodbye.* Navy finished the sentence in her head.

"I made you something," Jackson said. "If you want a little breakfast."

Navy took the hand Jackson offered and stood up. "You? Made food?"

"Don't sound so shocked." The bags under Jackson's eyes countered his smile, "Also . . . I may have burned breakfast."

Jackson had set the table with two cups of coffee and two plates. Two pastries popped out of the toaster. The edges were a very dark brown and smoking just a little bit. "Cinnamon-roll-flavored toaster things. Best I could do," Jackson apologized. "Even Giraldi's isn't open this early."

He put the pastries on her plate, then put two more in for himself.

Navy sat down and nibbled at her breakfast. While Jackson's back was turned, she discreetly broke off the worst bits and hid them with her napkin.

"How is it?" Jackson asked after he sat down.

"The coffee's perfect," Navy said. He had put in exactly as much cream and sugar as she liked.

"Guess I'm more of a barista than a chef," Jackson said. "I can try again?" He was already getting up; Navy pressed down on his hand to keep him sitting.

"I appreciate the thought," Navy said. "Relax." *I don't care about food. I just want you here.*

"What I said at the gym." Jackson tapped a finger against the table. "About you making me feel guilty for doing my job. I'm sorry. Again. I wasn't being fair to you."

"I wasn't being fair either," Navy said. "I should have asked whether you wanted to go to North Korea before I refused to send the message."

"You were trying to protect me."

"Like when you told Byron I shouldn't go on the Hackerville op. Whether or not I went to Hackerville wasn't your decision." Navy sipped her coffee. "And this operation . . . it's not my decision whether or not you should go. We both made the same mistake." Two years together, and still Navy felt like navigating a relationship was like stumbling around in the dark. "We should be better at this by now."

Jackson shrugged. "We're human. I haven't had a lot of practice. Being in a long-term relationship, I mean."

Navy had always thought of Jackson as the functional one.

"I—" Jackson looked guilty. "My job means I'm gone a lot. I don't think I handled it as well as I could have. None of my relationships lasted very long, and eventually I just gave up."

"That's a terrible excuse." Navy smiled wryly. "You're a psychologist. You're supposed to know how to handle messy emotions."

"I'm much better at giving other people advice," Jackson said.

Navy saw the clock and sobered. "You have to leave in five minutes."

Jackson nodded.

"I need you to come back," Navy said.

"Navy—"

"You're going to tell me I need to be prepared for the worst-case scenario." Navy finally knew what she had to say. "You're going to say I'm strong enough to make it without you. You're going to say I should find a way to be happy if you're gone. That you understand this is difficult for me and you're sorry."

"I—"

"I'm still figuring out how I can be me and you can be you and we can be us." She could feel herself tearing up and hated it. "I tried not to, but I love you. We get more than two years together. We have to. *I need you to come back.*"

"I'll come home," Jackson said. "I love you, Navy."

But Navy saw everything Jackson left unsaid in the creases of his forehead, in his stormy green eyes. Everything Navy knew already. Sometimes the world took things away from you without your permission. Because Navy needed the illusion of control, Jackson was making a promise he couldn't be sure he could keep. She needed to believe, for the next few minutes, if she wanted Jackson to come back and Jackson wanted to come back then Jackson would come back.

She walked Jackson to the door. She hugged him and they kissed. But as Jackson's hand slipped out of hers and the door closed, Navy already felt the illusion of control dissolving.

***

Min Gyu had to choose. Everything he would carry with him to America had to fit in the small shoulder bag he normally carried to work. Had to fit easily. He couldn't have risked applying for a travel permit, and that meant he couldn't be seen packing for a trip.

The few papers he needed to carry with him didn't take up much space: his birth certificate, his parent's marriage license. One photo of his parents taken on their wedding day in front of a Kim Il Sung statue, as most couples did.

But he wanted to take something more. Just one thing to remind him that in the midst of all the misery and wanting and pain, they had protected each other as best they could. A symbol of the rare, precious moments when his father had pointed out the wildflowers pushing their way through cracks in the sidewalk. Or when his mother had wrapped a warm multicolored scarf around his neck in the middle of a cold winter. She made the scarf from yarn scraps pulled out of the garbage behind the textile factory.

The scarf was threadbare now and too bulky to fit anyway. Min Gyu looked around his bedroom. The miniature replica tank he had played with as a child would fit. As a child, the toy had covered his palm. Now it fit easily in his fist. A red star inside a white circle was emblazoned on the side. A gift from Min Gyu's uncle, Sung Yong, when they had still gathered for family dinners.

"No!" Min Gyu's mother had said, when his father was about to throw it out. "Sung Yong will notice."

His mother had carefully set it on the shelf with Min Gyu's other toys. "Do you remember the story of the white tiger?" she asked Min Gyu.

Every North Korean child knew that the white tiger was an enormous beast that lived in the Kumgang mountains and tormented the nearby villagers.

"When you are hunting a White Tiger, you must have patience," his mother said. "The first shot cannot miss." Even at eight years old, Min Gyu had understood. She meant they would only get one chance to defect. Discovery meant life in a prison camp.

Min Gyu opened his fist to see the imprint of the toy against his palm. He slipped the tank inside a small pocket inside his bag. He had waited ten years since his father's death and his mother's imprisonment. Min Gyu had been patient. And now he had his one shot. He would not miss. He could not miss. He could not save them now, but he could save himself. The ghosts of his parents would finally rest when Min Gyu's feet were on American soil.

Chapter 13

The military transport to South Korea had all the discomforts of commercial travel plus some. After ten hours on a seat with no padding, Jackson's ass had gone numb. The net that formed the backrest dug into his neck. And his knees were butted up against boxes of supplies for Camp Red Cloud the plane had picked up during a stop in Portland. He was glad, at least, for the roar of the engines that made it hard to think too much. He'd crossed too many time zones and had too little sleep to think clearly. Almost twenty hours ago, he'd said goodbye to Navy. In another few hours, he'd land in South Korea.

Jackson bundled his jacket into a pillow and tried to sleep, again. He failed, again. On the other side of the plane, Saul wasn't sleeping much either. In Saul's less-guarded moments, Jackson saw nausea mixed with fear. Perhaps Saul was regretting his insistence on being there to witness the operation firsthand.

Kevin was sleeping fine, despite the turbulence. Jackson read the packing labels on the shrink-wrapped pallets scraping at his knees in the hope it would put him to sleep. The hours only passed more slowly. When Jackson felt the landing gear drop, he knew he'd be doing this operation more on adrenaline than sleep. Kevin stirred just as the wheels hit the runway.

The pilot came back to the cargo area after they had landed. "You said you wanted to be discreet," she said to Kevin. Then to all of them, "You'll want to get off now if you don't want to be seen by the soldiers unloading the plane." She didn't ask where her passengers were going or why secrecy was important. Jackson appreciated the professionalism.

Jackson, Kevin, and Saul were dressed in standard army uniforms to blend in. Once they left the runway, no one would give them a second look as they walked across the base.

A large jeep, engine already running, was waiting for them at the entrance. The sun's rays glinted off a wedding ring on the driver's hand. The climate was as humid as a summer in DC. Jackson was relieved to climb into the air-conditioned jeep. Saul squeezed himself into the back seat with two other men in plain clothes – the rest of the insertion team. Jackson knew from the mission briefing they were Green Berets. Once they were off base, everyone would change into civilian clothes.

The driver turned the wheel toward an imposing front gate with a guard's house. The sliver of countryside beyond was lush and green. The driver rolled down his window and waved at the guard. A section of the barbed wire-topped fence rolled open.

A blonde woman occupied the front seat – another soldier? Even in profile, with Jackson nearly blinded by the setting sun, she seemed familiar. Erin. The same Erin who promised she would deliver his last wishes to Navy.

"Did you know about this?" Jackson demanded of Kevin.

Kevin snapped his seatbelt into place. "She's here to help. We can use her skills. Get over it."

The Green Berets on either side of Saul shifted as he leaned forward to study Erin. "I didn't authorize this. Who is she?"

"Your best chance of looking good," Kevin said.

"I'm the commander on this mission—"

Kevin cut him off with a laugh. "That guy to your left is a commander. You haven't left the office in ten years."

Saul looked around the car for support but found none. "Turn the car around," Saul said. "We're taking her back."

The driver didn't even slow down.

"You accused *me* of being power-hungry?" Saul was gripping Jackson's seat in one hand and Kevin's in the other. "You're the one trying to take over."

Jackson recognized Kevin's smile. It meant he was one step ahead.

"Actually, I'm not." Kevin pointed to the bulky man to the left of Saul. "You're the one who sent the email requesting Commander Garrett here be put in charge of the mission and that Erin be added to the team."

"But I didn't ..." Saul's confusion was short-lived. "You asked Navy. When I get back, I'll have her head."

Kevin shrugged. "Your superiors were impressed with your willingness to sacrifice control for the good of the mission. After all, Commander Garrett's team knows the territory. But if you want to explain how someone accessed your email because you had a remote home security camera pointed at your 2FA token and all your passwords were based on information posted on your Facebook page, that's your call."

Navy hadn't told Jackson anything about taking over Saul's email account. Probably better that Jackson hadn't known what Navy was doing. Jackson didn't like when Navy put herself at risk for him. Silly, he knew. And contradictory. One of the things he loved about her was how tenaciously she fought to protect the people she loved.

"We'll do our mission briefing on the way," Commander Garrett said. The corners of his eyes wrinkled, though he didn't smile. "This operation was a bit rushed."

Saul's neck turned red. "I don't think I need to tell you how important—"

"We understand," Garrett said. "That's why my unit volunteered. We're supposed to be on R&R right now."

"It's common for soldiers to volunteer if they really believe in the mission," Jackson said. Perhaps a little guilt would be good for Saul.

"Our driver and translator is a South Korean soldier assigned to Camp Red Cloud. Also a volunteer," Garrett added.

"We know what neutralizing North Korea means to the Americans," the driver said. "Imagine what it means to us."

"I get it," Saul said. "I get it."

Jackson figured that was as close to an apology as Saul could do. An uncomfortable silence stretched out the minutes while rolling green hills dotted with farms and rice paddies passed by outside. Colorful wildflowers decorated the fields. It was, if one could concentrate on it, beautiful. At the moment, Jackson was worried Saul's ego would test the group's patience. Better to change the subject.

"You didn't say your name," Jackson said to the driver.

"Seong-Hun Park. You can call me Sunny," the driver said. "Americans can never get my name right." Sunny smiled as he said this, but Jackson wondered if the man ever tired of adjusting his name for foreigners. Garrett and his team seemed to get along well with Sunny, but the power imbalance between South Korea and the United States would always color the relationship between soldiers of military allies. South Korea needed the United States much more than the other way around.

Garrett pointed to the soldier on the other side of Saul. "This is my intelligence officer, Bradley. Southeast Asia is his specialty."

Bradley had a small mouth and large eyes. His long lashes made his face seem doll-like, in contrast to his muscled form. His eyes betrayed a carefully hidden eagerness. "Glad to be here."

"Erin Brody is our ... what was your official title again?"

The commander and Erin grinned at a shared joke.

"Liaison on extraordinary subject termination techniques," she said. Translated: Erin was here because she was good at killing people.

"My team knows your résumé, Kevin," Garrett said. "And Jackson, given your service record, may I say that the army is happy to have you back as a soldier for the next couple days."

Jackson appreciated Garrett's leadership style. No bluster and a focus on group cohesiveness.

"In case it wasn't made clear to you, this is a very sensitive and dangerous mission," Garrett continued. That last statement was probably for Saul's benefit. "The United States has no formal diplomatic relations with North Korea. If you are captured inside the country, extraction will be difficult to impossible. Brutal and inhumane conditions are the norm for prisoners in North Korea, and that's for their own people. You can expect worse. We must be invisible. Foreigners are rare outside of the capital and are expected to travel with North Korean handlers. If we are separated, do not trust any locals."

Bradley stepped into the commander's rehearsed pause. "The people have been taught to hate Americans. The ones who don't hate you should be too scared to help you. If someone is eager to help you, you should assume they are going to turn you in."

The one aspect of undercover work Jackson had the most difficulty explaining to junior agents was the grueling combination of banality and terror. Right now, the fate of the United States diplomacy with North Korea rested on the shoulders of seven people riding in an unmarked jeep on the same roads families used to travel to weddings and farmers used to deliver their goods.

"You three need to change into civilian clothes before we get to the Imjingang train station. Once we reach the train station, our cover is a tourist group visiting Peace Park." Garrett reached for some plastic bags on the floor and tossed one to Jackson, Kevin and Saul. "Operations support got these outfits to match your cover."

Inside Jackson's bag was a pair of jeans in his size and a long-sleeve button-up shirt with a matching undershirt. The tennis shoes were also his size but weren't new. A nice touch, Jackson admitted. He wouldn't look like he'd just stepped out of a department store. He unbuckled his seatbelt and unzipped his army-issue boots. He pulled his pants off as best he could in the cramped interior.

Kevin was doing the same. Saul held his clothes in his hands, eyeing them uncertainly. The plastic bag crunched as it shifted when the car followed the curving highway. Jackson almost felt sorry for him. Saul was out of his element, and he knew it.

"Did you want a changing room?" asked Garrett pointedly. "We don't have time to stop. It's a two-hour drive and we have to get to the tunnel before dark."

"I'll close my eyes," Erin promised.

Jackson shot her a look. He didn't like Saul any more than Erin did, but alienating him would just make him posture more. Jackson put his uniform into the empty plastic bag and leaned back. He really should sleep; he hadn't gotten any rest on the plane. The next time Jackson looked up, the gleaming high rises of a city were in the distance.

"Paju," Sunny was saying. "Fancy apartments for cheap. If you don't mind being within range of the North Korean artillery on the other side of the River of the Dead."

"River of the Dead?" Jackson was sorry he asked before he'd finished the question. Uncomfortable memories from

Greek mythology surfaced. He half expected to see a wooden boat with a hooded ferryman.

"During the last famine in North Korea, bodies washed down the river all the time. Mostly stopped after the nineties."

The more Jackson learned about the Korean peninsula, the less he wanted to know. He eyed the bridge they were approaching. "So we're going to cross the River of the Dead."

Sunny winked. "Sort of."

Just before they reached the bridge, Sunny took a sharp right into a brightly lit train station. A friendly blue sign said "Imjingang" in English and Korean. The parking lot was sparsely occupied. Jackson checked his watch.

"We're tourists," Garrett said as the car's headlights went dark. "Out for a late walk in the Peace Park." He grinned. "Just imagine we're one big happy family on vacation. And follow my lead."

Jackson hoped Saul's glare wouldn't be visible on binoculars. The driver's door opened and Sunny hopped out. He wore a T-shirt with 'Foreigner DMZ tours' emblazoned on the front. So Sunny was their "tour guide."

Garrett's demeanor changed the second before he stepped out. He dropped the posture of leader and instead looked around, as if he were a little lost. Then he smiled at Sunny. The smile was superficial, the kind shared between strangers passing on the street. The sun wasn't even down and Jackson felt a chill in the air. He'd forgotten how far north North Korea was.

Sunny clapped a hand on Saul's back, still smiling. "They're watching, my friend. Play along."

Erin looped her arm through Jackson's as part of the charade, as casually as if they'd been together for years. He forced himself to follow Sunny's advice and smiled at Erin.

"You lied to me," Jackson said.

She shook her head. "I said I'd take care of it. Byron has your precious box. And now I'm here, taking care of it."

Jackson concentrated on following Sunny. They walked a short distance up the road. Here was another parking lot, but this one was half full of buses and vans with various tour company logos on them. Jackson guessed there was a sign somewhere in Korean forbidding parking personal vehicles. Sunny led them to a gray building labeled "North Korea Center" in English, with Korean characters next to it. Inside, large displays with black-and-white photographs educated a handful of milling tourists.

Sunny motioned for them to look around. "I set up a special tour." While Jackson, now thankfully separated from Erin, pondered the inhumanities happening beyond the soldiers and barbed wire in the photos, Sunny talked briefly with someone at the information desk.

Key in hand, Sunny returned and gathered them together. "We have a video presentation in this room." They walked down a short hallway, and then Sunny opened a thick metal door labeled only in Korean. Chairs were lined up in neat rows. Saul was the last to enter; Jackson heard a lock click into place automatically as the door shut. Before the echo of the click had faded, Garrett assumed the air of a commander again.

"Bradley, lead the way," Garrett said.

Where was the tunnel? Jackson wondered. His question was answered as Sunny opened another door whose label Jackson couldn't read. He smelled damp and oil and echoes. As ordered, Bradley and Erin went first. Jackson followed, aware of Kevin's quiet steps following. The calm of experience had fallen over them. Focus on the job. Thinking about what might go wrong was only a distraction. Failure was always possible, but it was best not to dwell on it.

The concrete basement hallway was lined with brightly colored pipes labeled in the loops, circles, and lines of Korean. Several turns and locks and doors later, Jackson found himself in a small room with two South Korean soldiers. Between Jackson, Erin, Kevin, and Bradley the room was nearly full.

An underground border crossing. That was Jackson's first impression. A South Korean soldier at a desk with the paraphernalia to examine documents: a desk light, a scanner, and a small metal tube that was probably a black light. Cameras on every corner so no one could enter or leave without being identified. Another South Korean soldier stood at attention on the other side of the room.

Sunny winked at Jackson. "We're not going over the river. We're going under."

"The rest of your team is at the entrance," the South Korean soldier at the desk told Bradley, handing over a stack of white plastic cards. "Your access cards are good for forty-eight hours. You know the drill. You can't make it back by then, good luck."

If the comment unnerved Bradley, he didn't show it.

Jackson scanned the room; Saul and Garrett were still missing. A second later Saul entered with Garrett close behind him. Neither looked happy. A look passed between Garrett and Bradley. Garrett shrugged. Jackson recognized the gesture. Garrett had been overruled and couldn't make a big deal about it without breaking the command structure. He had probably tried to convince Saul to stay behind. It was the wise thing to do. But Saul didn't trust Kevin any more than Kevin trusted him.

"We're set, Commander," Bradley said. Again, Bradley led the way. A thin line of lights along the top of a sloping wall led down, down, down. Jackson heard Bradley mutter under his breath "Abandon all hope, ye who enter here."

"Did the North Koreans dig this tunnel or did we?" Jackson asked.

Bradley's quiet laugh echoed off the rough stone walls. "It was a joint effort."

In the past couple weeks, Jackson had done some reading. There were four tunnels under the border that South Korea had publicly acknowledged discovering. North Korea claimed all of them were built for peaceful mining. But it was widely believed that North Korea wasn't technically capable of tunneling under the Imjin river.

The steps were slippery with moisture, and the metal banister creaked under Jackson's hand.

"The South Korean government found the tunnel about ten years ago based on vibrations reported by our soldiers," Sunny said. "We let it leak that we were investigating possible tunnels in the area and construction stopped. The North Koreans have never acknowledged the tunnel. The South Koreans don't want to."

Jackson thought that nothing could be more complicated than the tribal politics of Afghanistan. Apparently, he was wrong. "Why not? It's a clear breach of the armistice."

"Exactly," Sunny agreed.

As Bradley turned, his face was illuminated in the wan light. "It was during the Sunshine Policy, when Lee Myung-bak was trying to make peace. If South Korea had acknowledged the tunnel, then they would have had to do something about it. So the military decided to make use of it."

Their shoes scratched against the grit on the steps. They were still headed down, and by the looks of it, they would be for a while longer. Jackson was not normally claustrophobic, but he could feel the weight of water and stone above them.

"You should feel special, Jackson," Erin said from somewhere behind him. "The commander says there's only about a hundred people in the world who know about the tunnel. And now you're one of them."

Jackson thought of Navy, at home feeling guilty and worried and waiting for news. "Yeah, special. That's exactly how I feel."

The steps ended abruptly in a round cavern strafed with the vertical lines from explosives. Ten men were clustered around a thick steel door. Each man was built like Garrett and Bradley and wore casual civilian clothes.

"About time, Commander," drawled a man with red hair.

"Our weapons officer, Ozark," Garrett said. "See him for gear."

In the dim light, Jackson hadn't noticed the packs lined up along the wall. They were the kind of backpacks you might find left on the back-to-school sale rack after all the good ones had been taken. None of them had designs or patterns of any sort. All were dark colors.

Bradley gave five cards to Ozark, then distributed the rest among the waiting soldiers.

"Line up, tourists," Ozark said.

Surprisingly, Saul followed the order without complaint.

Ozark held up the cards and pointed to a slot near the heavy door. "These unlock the tunnel. After you slide your card in, you have forty-eight hours to return. Once we pass through the door, this card is more important than anything else I will give you. There is no other way home."

Erin took hers with a smile. Without breaking eye contact with Ozark, she tucked the card away in her bra. Kevin rolled his eyes at Erin and took his card. Saul's hand shook slightly as he took his. Jackson turned the cold plastic over in his hands. Blank on both sides. So the card couldn't be traced back to this tunnel . . . and the U.S. government could pretend they'd never sent Jackson in the first place.

"There's a pack for each of you with a few essentials, including gear for spending the night outside. Use the matches to start a campfire and I'll shoot you myself. We stay together – and invisible – at all times." He picked up the bag closest to him and gave it to Erin. "Yours has a broken-down sniper rifle, as requested." The next two packs went to Kevin and Jackson. "You two have pistols, we're not carrying anything bigger."

Walking into hostile territory without a high-capacity, automatic weapon made Jackson nervous, but he understood. Larger weapons were easier to see from a distance and harder to ditch if needed. Even the sniper rifle Erin carried was a risk.

"This isn't very big," Saul said, weighing his pack.

Ozark stared at him blankly. "Yeah."

"Well, I mean, is there a tent in there?"

"Sure." Ozark laughed. "And one of those plastic balls that makes ice cream while you're camping."

Garrett stepped in. "Survival camping supplies only. A thermal blanket and a little food to get you through. If we're seen from a distance, our mission won't be obvious. There's also a headlamp in there. I suggest you put it on."

"We sent Mole Man down the tunnel, sir," one of the soldiers said. "Everything looks quiet."

The commander nodded, but still looked troubled. "Guess it's time to go, then. You know what they say. You have to go out, you don't have to come back."

Jackson was surprised to hear a coast guard motto from an army commander.

"That's what your mother said," Ozark said with a grin.

"Damn right," Garrett said. "My mother was a coastie, through and through."

Rustling filled the cavern as everyone put on their packs and lined up, one by one. Ozark led the group. He inserted his card into the slot under the glowing red bar. The bar turned green and a massive lock inside the metal door clunked open. Even Ozark hesitated a second before swinging open what looked like a bank vault door. A cloud of dank air hit them. Perhaps it was Jackson's imagination, but he smelled death.

As they stepped into the dark tunnel, illuminated only by the streams of light from their headlamps, Jackson nearly tripped over a squat robot with treads instead of tires. A camera was mounted on a crane-like neck that could extend up and down.

"That's Mole Man," Garrett told Jackson. "We send him down the tunnel before every mission. Make sure it's clear. Then he comes back to his charging station and uploads the video to a screen on the other side."

"You still seem concerned," Jackson said.

The commander's light bounced off the ceiling and walls as he looked around. "Funny engineering story. The first time the North Koreans built a tractor it would only run backward."

Funny in another time or place, perhaps.

"So I can't decide which situation would be better: that the tunnel is being actively maintained, and I have to shoot a few people. Or if they've abandoned it and we're the only people who have seen this tunnel in years."

Jackson added tunnel collapse to the list of ways he might die on this operation. The tunnel height got shorter, and everyone had to stoop.

"Couldn't even feed their fucking soldiers," Ozark's drawl echoed. "My back's going to hurt for a week after this."

Of course. The tunnel was built with the average height of the North Korea soldier in mind.

The dark was not silent. Their breaths ricocheted off the uneven walls. The overlapping sounds played tricks with Jackson's ears. Their headlamps only shone so far ahead. Anything could be waiting in the absolute darkness beyond.

Chapter 14

"Headlamps off." The whispered command passed down the line in the tunnel. Jackson knew that Ozark must have seen the exit, even though Jackson could not. Jackson's eyes adjusted to the dimness of the tunnel exit as he followed the shuffling footsteps forward. The first thing he would do when they could stand up straight was find some aspirin. Hours of walking stooped over had tied a knot in his lower back.

Garrett turned and held up a hand. Jackson obeyed, stopping behind the semicircle of soldiers at the exit. Beyond the ends of their guns, a forest slept in twilight. Jackson's breath fogged the air. He hadn't expected the countryside to look like a picture from a storybook. North Korea's nonfunctional economy meant development had left many areas to nature.

Garrett signaled for Ozark, Erin, and Bradley to scout the blind corners at the exit. Erin's face was quiet and focused. This was her zone. Save for her smaller build, nothing distinguished her from the Green Berets. The three crept forward, kneeling more than walking. Their heads turned as they studied the gray, shifting limbs of the trees, right and left. Then again. After a long minute, Ozark motioned for everyone to follow. A break in the leaves marked the trail. Saul tried to walk next to the soldier in front of him but was nudged into the single file line. When he drifted too close again, Garrett yanked him back.

"Line formation," Garrett said. "Match the others."

The spacing minimized casualties in the event of surprise attacks. The forest seemed to thin as light tinged the horizon. Their cover was eroding. Jackson, and everyone else, scanned the area more intensely the more exposed they became. Soon he heard an engine idling in the distance. There should be a truck waiting for them on a dirt road a half-mile away. When they were close enough to see the truck, Ozark dug a flashlight out of his pocket, his finger hesitating on the button.

The truck idling on the road might be their transport. Or it might be just a truck, and signaling with the flashlight would reveal their position.

Ozark blinked the flashlight three times. The headlights of the truck flashed twice. Ozark motioned the group forward again, across the open ground between the trees and the road. An early dawn speared the land with long shadows. They were sitting ducks, if anyone cared to look.

A wiry man hopped out of the truck as they approached. A Ural-4320, similar to the beat-up trucks used by mercenaries and smugglers the world over. The driver smiled, displaying his missing teeth. Sunny shook the driver's hand and said something in Korean. An envelope changed hands. Half of the driver's payment for bringing them further inland.

When Jackson saw the cargo area, he wondered if Sunny had made a mistake. Under the tarp, the truck looked full of cardboard boxes labeled in Chinese. Ozark pushed Jackson aside and reached into a space between the boxes and a door swung wide. Shells of cardboard boxes had been glued to the door to hide a cargo area with benches inside. Some of the smaller boxes even opened. Good cover, but with the tarp and the subterfuge, inside the truck was nearly as dark as the tunnel.

Erin hopped in without hesitation. Saul had to be pushed in. Jackson hauled himself into the bed of the truck. He settled on yet another uncomfortable seat, used his flashlight to dig through his pack, and swallowed two aspirin.

"Do you trust the driver?" Jackson whispered to Sunny. Sunny shrugged. "More or less."

Another question Jackson wished he hadn't asked. Every smuggler in the world lived in legal limbo between lawful society and black markets. Some smugglers used that flexibility as a cover for their resistance against the government in charge. Some smugglers just liked the profit. Jackson knew how difficult it was to figure out who to trust in hostile territory.

The truck bounced along the scarred roads. Metal joints creaked under their feet as the tires kicked up gravel with sharp pings. Pinpricks of light broke through the tarp. It was a welcome sight until the temperature inside the truck rose. Jackson felt moist circles forming in his armpits and behind his knees. For a truck that wasn't hiding, the 136-mile drive to Onchon would take two hours or so. Using the back roads and smuggling routes, it would take all day.

Garrett's men talked in low whispers, exchanging dirty jokes mixed with stories of home. None seemed to regret voluntarily giving up their leave for one more mission. Their interaction made it clear that Erin, Jackson, Saul, and Kevin were outsiders. Saul had developed a facial tic that made Jackson think Saul was regretting his decision to come. Another oncoming engine passed them, then turned around and began to follow. Conversation stopped. Garrett pressed his lips together.

"Just be quiet," Sunny whispered to them. "This happens sometimes."

"How often exactly?" Kevin asked, readying his weapon.

"Well, this is only the second time."

Erin scanned the incomprehensible labels on the boxes under the benches. "Any of these containers we should be worried about shooting?"

Sunny shook his head.

Garrett waved his hand in front of their faces. "*Only* on my signal."

Men yelled. The smuggler turned the engine off. Boots crunched in dirt. Jackson knew the sound of military boots anywhere. Of course, a good portion of the male population in North Korea was in the military. The people who stopped them could be anyone from the state police to a lowly patrol. The driver's door opened, then shut.

The North Korean soldiers barked something at the driver, and the voices moved to the back of the truck. "They want to inspect the cargo," Sunny whispered.

Garrett's men had arranged their guns to cover anyone standing behind the truck. The driver would certainly be killed in the crossfire, if it came to that.

The driver said something in a tone of voice that sounded more like a sales pitch than a plea.

"He's asking them what their favorite shows are," Sunny whispered.

Jackson heard a cardboard box open and hands digging through the contents. Something spilled. The insulting tone of the North Korean soldiers was answered with something that sounded like obsequious praise from the smuggler.

Sunny covered his mouth to keep from laughing.

Garrett's tension turned to annoyance. "What now?"

"Their favorite show is the *Real Housewives of New Jersey*. They just took a whole season. Our driver is complimenting their taste."

Garrett signaled his men to stand down once the truck was back on the road. Jackson and the team had just been saved by a reality TV show.

Chapter 15

Kevin was more than ready to reach the factory where they would meet Min Gyu. They had now been in the truck for four hours and would be here for another six at least. They ate food from their packs. They drank water and pissed in the empty bottles. Garrett allowed sleeping in shifts. It was getting dark again when they reached their final stop. Kevin took deep breaths of fresh, chilled air. The patches of sweat on his clothes had dried, leaving the fabric stiff and scratchy.

"You stay in the truck," Garrett said to Saul.

"But—"

The commander leaned in ominously. "We can do this the easy way or the embarrassing way," he said quietly. "But I am *not* letting you get my men killed because of some sort of power trip."

Saul glared but backed down.

"You have a very important job," Garrett said. "You and Sunny are going to make sure our ride is still here when we get back."

Meaning, Sunny was going to make sure the smuggler didn't run away and Saul was going to twiddle his thumbs.

"Earpieces, everyone," Garrett ordered. The small plastic earpieces were the same sort Kevin used on his own missions. Everyone would be able to talk to everyone else. One by one, he had everyone test their com. Then he motioned for Kevin, Jackson, and Erin to come closer. "Your night vision is in your headlamp. Just turn the light off, fold down the visor, and hit the button."

The headlamps had seemed bulky to Kevin, but he would have never guessed what they were hiding. It was ingenious. He made a mental note to get them for his team on their next mission.

"Try to ditch the headlamps if you're captured," Garrett said. "This is new tech."

While they walked the last mile, Kevin reviewed what they would find at the pickup point. From the satellite pictures, he knew the terrain surrounding the abandoned steel factory held no advantages for them. Five hundred yards of bare ground bordered the factory on all sides. Anyone in the factory would see them coming.

Erin separated from the group as they approached the clearing around the factory. She would be covering them with the sniper rifle from the treetops. Garrett stopped the group by holding up his hand. Ozark and Bradley split off in separate directions, staying under the cover of the trees. The team had approached on the southeast side of the building, where the only entrance was. Ozark and Bradley were scouting the areas of the clearing Erin couldn't see.

Ten minutes later, Kevin's earpiece crackled to life with Erin's voice. "In position. Southeast side is clear."

Ozark and Bradley returned soon after. "All clear," both reported.

It was too damn easy, Kevin thought. Too quiet.

Garrett frowned, no doubt thinking the same thing. "Let's go," Garrett said.

Jackson, gun drawn, fell into formation with Garrett's team, as if he had worked with them for months. Kevin followed suit.

Kevin was trying not to focus on how naked he felt. He understood why Garrett had chosen to outfit the mission with limited weapons, but he didn't like the tradeoff. Dry grass bent and crackled under their feet. They were halfway to the sagging factory now, halfway to relative safety.

Only a few more yards. As Kevin got closer, he could see there was no door. Just a gaping, dark rectangle. A few more feet now.

Garrett pointed at three of the men on his team. "Keep our exit clear," Garrett told them quietly.

Kevin flipped down his night vision goggles to scan the room before entering. He saw no signs of life. Not even any footprints on the concrete floor. Though he wasn't sure there would be. Grease and dirt had mixed with the rust he could taste in the air to coat the floor by the entrance.

On Garrett's command, the team followed Kevin into the building. Hulking, broken machinery stalked the interior. Everything that could be carried away and sold for scrap had been carried away a long time ago. Jackson looked at Kevin with a grim expression. Garrett didn't look any happier than they did.

Too quiet.

Either Min Gyu hadn't made it, or they had just sprung a trap.

"See if there are any other rooms," Garrett ordered. "Then let's get the fuck out of here."

They fanned out to walk along each wall. Without Sunny, no one could read the signs. Kevin found one empty office with a wooden desk that had been left to rot.

Then a door, where an arc of dust had been swept clear. "Someone's here," Kevin said. "East side, far corner."

"Cover a line to the exit," Kevin heard Garrett say through the earpiece. "Jackson, you're up."

"Me first," Kevin told Jackson.

The door screeched on its hinges, and against Kevin's nerves. Sympathetic scraps of metal picked up the frequency, humming. He wished the damn building would shut up and let him concentrate.

Kevin stepped into an auditorium with rows of chairs bolted to the floor. He could imagine the workers filing in, pulling down the seats and leaning against the wooden chair backs for the morning indoctrination.

The beam of a flashlight blinded Kevin in the eye with the night vision goggle. Kevin blinked away stars. A man had appeared on the stage. Must be Min Gyu. Around the edges of the flashlight beam, Kevin could see ratty curtains swaying on stage right.

"You're not Jackson," Min Gyu said. He paced nervously, gripping the canvas strap of a bag slung over his shoulder. "Where's Jackson?"

"I'm here." Jackson hurried through the door, tearing off his headlamp. He walked into the wide center aisle, so Min Gyu could see him clearly. "Follow me," Jackson said to Min Gyu.

A shuffling, scratching, squeaking sound came from behind Min Gyu, who turned, startled. Jackson and Kevin both raised their guns. Then the sound multiplied. Boots pounded in from behind Min Gyu. Twenty men, then forty, then sixty with weapons drawn. In the back, a man pointed at Kevin and yelled something. Kevin guessed it was Korean for "Get him, too."

The soldiers hadn't overtaken Jackson yet. Kevin fired several shots and watched three men fall. Then Kevin ducked, expecting return fire. Despite all the gun waving, none of the North Korean soldiers fired. They wanted their prisoners alive and were willing to lose as many men as necessary. Kevin resumed shooting and took two strides toward Jackson. A shot rang out near his feet, but not from the direction of the North Koreans. It was a warning shot from Jackson, telling Kevin to stay away.

Jackson's calculus was correct. Two pistols were no match for the sixty men surging through the auditorium.

Even with the whole team, it was no contest. Kevin was close enough to the door to back out. Jackson was trapped.

"Abort, abort," Kevin heard himself say, even as he took another step forward. "Overwhelming force. Evacuate."

A high-ranking man stood proudly next to Min Gyu on stage. Min Gyu was shaking, terrified. Green uniforms swarmed like rats over Jackson, knocking him to the floor. A green uniform came for Kevin, reaching out to grab his arm. Amateur. Kevin grabbed the soldier's arm and jerked it back until he heard the shoulder dislocate. Then Kevin shot him in the face. The bullet took out the next soldier in line too, but Kevin didn't kid himself.

I have to go. I have to leave Jackson behind. The seething green mass of soldiers had swallowed Jackson. They were kicking him, but Kevin could no longer hear Jackson's grunts over the collective bloodlust.

Kevin shot two more soldiers reaching for him, then backed out and slammed the door.

"Cover me!" Ozark shouted.

Kevin emptied his gun into the door, while Ozark shoved something in the crack at the bottom. Then Kevin and Ozark ran. The delay might give them enough time to escape. If the North Koreans were still set on sacrificing their own soldiers to capture prisoners alive.

There was no time to chart a path through the debris. Kevin leapt over an oddly shaped square and caught his toe on the corner. He could feel he had broken it. He gritted his teeth and kept running, urged on by the pounding feet of Garrett's team around him.

"Nasties coming from the northeast to cut you off at the door," Erin reported in Kevin's ear. Her sniper rifle cracked in the background. "Run faster."

"Sunny, come in," Garrett said between pants.

"Here," Sunny replied.

"Our ride ready?"

"Whenever you get your lazy asses here."

Erin's sniper rifle cracked twice more as Kevin reached the clearing. Four uniformed bodies lay face down in the grass. Two hundred yards to reach the forest. One hundred. The group reached the trees, and Erin's rifle was still silent.

Garrett stopped the group briefly to scan the clearing. "Erin, come down."

"No, I can cover you."

"We only have one ride out of here. I need you on it." He looked at the sinister factory, the opening gaping like a rotten tooth. "I'm not losing anyone else today."

"Losing?"

Garrett was running again when he answered. "Get your ass to the truck. Now."

It was the fastest mile Kevin had ever run. The back door of the truck was open when they reached the road. They filled the interior with the smell of sweat and fear. The truck took off with Erin on the bumper, Garrett pulling her in.

"Where's Min Gyu? What's going on?" Saul asked.

Kevin let his control go. *"Where's Min Gyu?* Not here. Because it was a trap."

"A wha—"

Kevin slammed Saul against the side of the truck. "The North Koreans knew. They got Jackson. They fucking *knew*."

Saul's eyes widened as he realized who else was missing. "I'm sorry ... about Jackson."

Kevin let Saul go and fell back into his seat. In all of Kevin's years at the agency, he'd never lost an agent. He'd become cocky. Kevin thought it was his skill and his experience and his careful planning that had brought his people home. Turns out it was dumb luck. And of all the people to lose, Jackson. The line between friend and coworker had blurred a long time ago."

Erin threw a spent rifle magazine against the floor. It bounced and skittered as the bumpy road carried them farther and farther away. "What happened?"

"They were waiting for us in the auditorium. There were at least sixty, maybe more." Kevin saw the tight group, the backs of their uniforms shifting like the scales of one giant organism, Jackson falling under their weight.

"Evacuating without Jackson was the right call," Garrett said.

Kevin shook his head. "I'm not sure Navy will agree." He had made a promise to her. It never occurred to Kevin that he wouldn't be able to keep it.

***

Garrett organized the soldiers into shifts to let people sleep. Kevin didn't bother trying. His mouth tasted sour. His toe throbbed, jolted by every bump in the road. The adrenaline that had masked Kevin's grief was gone. There was no one to be angry at but himself, even though he knew he couldn't have done anything differently.

This was the job. Jackson knew it and accepted it. Kevin would have to as well. But tonight, he couldn't shake the feeling he was a coward. He was running away from a fight. A fight he couldn't win, certainly. But he was still running.

Eight torturous hours later, they arrived at the drop-off point. Garrett stirred Ozark awake. They gathered their weapons and packs, using their headlamps to search for anything they might have left behind.

Kevin's legs protested the second his feet hit the ground. The hard run, followed by a long confinement, had painfully tightened his muscles. Eight hours of trying to think of a way to rescue Jackson and not coming up with anything left him frustrated and beyond tired. Sunny pulled out another thick envelope. Whatever Sunny said as he handed it over upset the driver. Unconsciously, Kevin reached for his weapon. Garrett stopped his arm.

"Sunny's offering the driver asylum," Garrett said. "The North Koreans might be able to link his truck to the incident at the factory today."

Sunny pulled up his sleeve, to show his watch to the driver. Then Sunny pulled a treat wrapped in plastic out of his pack. Kevin had eaten one on the plane ride to base. Some sort of moon pie rip-off.

The driver backed away, waving his hands. He looked around at Kevin and the rest of Garrett's team, as if the driver wanted them all to hear. "I not come with you." His English was better than Kevin expected. "I not just ... smuggler."

"They'll be looking for you," Sunny said. "You have no family left here. Come with us, and we can set you up with a new life in South Korea. Everyone can afford a watch there and you'll have enough food."

"I know, I know." The driver smiled sadly. "Why you think I do this?"

"You've done us a great service today," Sunny said. "We are in your debt."

"It is ... duty." The driver scanned their confused faces and tried again. He pointed at the boxes on his truck. "Not just shows and movies for fun. Learns people that life is different. That our leader lies."

Sunny held out a hand, bowing slightly. "At the end of hardship comes happiness."

The driver answered in Korean. Sunny nodded and walked away.

"He won't come," Sunny told Garrett. "We should head back."

"Goddamnit," Garrett said. "Everyone, move out."

Kevin walked beside Sunny. "The last thing you said to the driver. About hardship. It meant something to him."

"It's a Korean proverb. I can't think of an exact equivalent in English. Maybe something about hard work and practice creating your own luck."

Kevin smiled bitterly. Creating his own luck, indeed. "If I make a chance to rescue Jackson, do you have a way to contact the driver?"

"Garrett or I can get you the driver," Sunny said. "But that's the least of your problems now."

"I know," Kevin said. "Believe me, I know."

Garrett had overheard. "If you make a chance, count us in."

Chapter 16

Jackson knew he would be captured the second he saw the rows of black boots pouring off the stage. He heard shots to his left, from Kevin. Three soldiers fell and were trampled by the rest. "Get out!" he yelled at Kevin.

Instead, Kevin came closer. Jackson felt for his earpiece and found nothing. A black spot on the floor answered his question. His earpiece had come out when he pulled off his headlamp. The soldiers were twenty feet away now. They had feverish eyes, eager for violence. He tried to catch Kevin's eye to wave him off, but Kevin was too focused on the threat.

Jackson turned his weapon and fired at the ground in front of Kevin. Finally, Kevin stopped advancing. As they looked at each other, Jackson saw Kevin coming to the same conclusion Jackson had. He dropped the headlamp, hoping Garrett's tech would be destroyed by trampling feet.

Jackson couldn't be saved.

Kevin had to leave.

The soldiers were ten feet away now. Jackson wondered whether he should turn his gun on himself, and in that second a thousand hands pressed down and held him to the floor.

More shots fired. As the first kick connected with his ribs, Jackson hoped the shots were Kevin's. A door slammed, locking Kevin out or in. Jackson couldn't tell. A bramble of arms and legs pummeled him on all sides, starbursts of pain exploding from everywhere. Instinct and training told him to curl up and protect his head.

The hatred was palpable. The soldiers weren't just doing their duty. They were slaying a devil.

A voice yelled with authority, and Jackson was hauled to his feet by hands that dug into his fresh bruises. He realized he could walk, mostly. A sharp pain near his kidney told him he had a broken rib. Even as Jackson catalogued his injuries, he had no delusions about the seriousness of his condition. It was easy to die of things you couldn't feel.

With effort, Jackson raised his head. Min Gyu was next to two grinning men. The number of bars on their uniforms told Jackson they were high ranking. They were talking, but Jackson couldn't understand a word. Even though the tone was congratulatory, Min Gyu looked terrified.

Was Min Gyu a victim here too? Or had he known the soldiers were here?. Jackson knew Min Gyu might have been coerced and tried to find compassion. He could not. All he could think of was how miserable the rest of his short life would be and how much Navy's heart would break when she heard the news.

Jackson stopped helping his captors and went limp They had to half-carry, half-drag him to a car. The rest of the soldiers milled around, waiting for their ride. He was thrown in the backseat, then bookended by two soldiers. Now was the time to attempt escaping, before he was behind walls and locked doors and prison fences. Because of his injuries from the beating, they hadn't bothered to restrain him. Jackson might be able to run. No, he told himself, he could run. Or at least he had to try.

On the next turn, Jackson used the centrifugal force to launch himself towards the door. He felt his hands touch the handle just before the butt of a gun connected with the base of his skull.

Jackson woke with a headache, tied to a chair in an interrogation room with grey cinderblock walls. The only light came from a strong overhead bulb in an exposed light fixture. He tested the knots binding his hands. Someone had done their job well. His ankles were tied to the chair legs. If he tipped the chair, he might be able to wiggle his arms free and work on the knots at his ankles. Maybe. If the effort didn't send his broken rib through his lung first.

A door opened and Min Gyu entered. He looked wrung out from fear. When the door shut behind him, he jumped.

Jackson tried to keep his face neutral. Min Gyu might be able to help him.

"What you must think of me." Min Gyu fumbled for something in his uniform pocket. A pack of cigarettes. He shook a lighter out of the crumpled pack. "I hope you don't mind?" But he lit the cigarette without waiting for an answer, breathing deeply until the end glowed red.

"You betrayed me." *Wrong move*, Jackson chastised himself. Whatever Min Gyu had done, the would-be defector was the only possible source of help inside this hellhole.

Min Gyu shook his head so emphatically Jackson was afraid Min Gyu might hurt himself. "No, no, no." Another deep drag of the cigarette, and still Min Gyu's hands shook. "I have to explain."

Jackson waited.

"I didn't know they were there. They ambushed me too. Stupid, stupid, stupid." Min Gyu pounded a fist against his leg. "I thought the auditorium would be safer, but they hid under the stage."

Min Gyu's story didn't make any sense. If Min Gyu had been caught trying to defect, he should be tied to an interrogation chair too—unless Min Gyu had been sent to extract information from Jackson, in return for lenient treatment.

Min Gyu sighed. "You don't believe me. Of course not. Why would you?"

The gray walls seemed to shift. What did Min Gyu want?

"Yung Bo works for State Security. He tries to find defectors. Yung Bo set up the ambush, then claimed I was helping with an operation to capture an American spy."

Random acts of kindness didn't match the reputation of State Security. "Why?" Jackson managed.

"Yung Bo wants to defect with me."

The story was a partial explanation for Min Gyu's behavior on stage with the two high-ranking men. "Yung Bo was on stage with you, when they took me away," Jackson said.

Min Gyu nodded.

Still, something didn't sound right. A man that high-ranking had resources. And would be a prize for South Korea. There were easier ways for a man with Yung Bo's privileges to defect.

An earnest face clouded by cigarette smoke leaned in toward Jackson. "I do not trust him either, but we have no choice."

Jackson tried not to cough and failed.

"I know, it's a terrible habit," Min Gyu said. "Hard to break here. My father taught me when I was ten." At Jackson's expression, Min Gyu's face hardened. "Don't judge him. He taught me to smoke to keep the hunger away when we had no food."

"I didn't mean anything," Jackson said. He couldn't quite manage an apology, given that Min Gyu was walking around and Jackson was tied to a chair.

"The good news is that Yung Bo will be overseeing your interrogation session. He will make sure there is no ... permanent damage."

Jackson waited for the punch line.

"The bad news is we must fake your death to get you out. Navy may not get my message before she hears the official news you are dead."

"And if we play along, Yung Bo will let us go." Jackson wasn't sure he bought Min Gyu's story, but he wasn't sure that mattered.

"That's what he says."

Jackson gritted his teeth. "I'm asking if you believe him."

Min Gyu shrugged. "You haven't lived here. You don't understand. Whether or not I believe him, we must do what he says."

The handle on the door turned and Min Gyu's neck jerked in that direction. "Remember, play along."

Jackson glared at Min Gyu's back as he bowed to Yung Bo, then scuttled out, face flickering between guilt and terror. How exactly was Jackson supposed to *play along*? Was he supposed to pretend to be hurting while Yung Bo tortured him?

Yung Bo entered with a younger man with fewer bars on his uniform. The younger man was wheeling a cart that would have fit nicely into any horror movie set. Gleaming metal instruments were neatly arranged on two trays. Jackson forced himself to catalogue them as potential weapons if he could get free. The assortment of pliers would be little use. The small knives and picks could be, but only if he were strategic in his strikes.

"Sometimes interrogations must be conducted with plausible deniability," Yung Bo said in English. "That is what we will practice today." Yung Bo picked up a long, sharp needle-like instrument from the cart. "A tool like this will leave marks that heal quickly but can inflict great pain."

Jackson wished he could think of a situation where things had been worse for him. He couldn't.

The young man took the needle-like instrument. His hands were unsteady. Maybe the propaganda hadn't taken root in his head, or maybe Jackson looked too weak to inspire hatred. Regardless, the young man looked every bit the devoted student as Yung Bo continued to explain technique. Yung Bo's sidelong glances and mischievous smile told Jackson that the lecture was as much about intimidating Jackson as it was about instructing the student.

Jackson summoned a memory. The first time he had danced with Navy. She had been wearing a long blue dress that glittered like the instrument now hovering next to his flesh. Pain fractured the image and Jackson summoned it again. Jackson was caught now, in that moment when their bodies were in sync with each other. He had wondered if her feelings matched his. *Don't you know?* she had said. *You've always made me nervous.*

He heard himself cry out, but distantly. His pulse kept tempo with the roaring in his ears. But even the pain from the needle being pushed slowly into his flesh couldn't dislodge her face from his mind. The young man was inexperienced. The torturer's apprentice didn't yet understand that even extreme pain required crescendos to truly be felt.

Chapter 17

Kevin hadn't slept since Jackson's capture. The military transport deposited fifteen weary fighters at the Army base outside DC. It had left with sixteen. Erin didn't look any better than Kevin felt.

"Do you need a ride home?" Kevin asked.

Erin raised her eyebrows. "You have a broken toe and you haven't slept in thirty hours. Maybe I should give you a ride home."

"Thirty-five hours and twenty-nine minutes," Kevin corrected. He knew exactly how long it had been since they had abandoned Jackson. "And you haven't slept either."

Saul approached hesitantly. "I'll handle the notification. In a few hours it will be morning."

Kevin shook his head. "No, I'll do it."

Disbelief flickered across Saul's face. "Have you done one before?" he asked gently.

The occasion had never come up before. "Navy should hear the news from me."

Erin cleared her throat. "Saul's right. You're not exactly known for your bedside manner."

Kevin was too tired to deal with Saul's interference. Even if Saul meant well. "Navy's mean when she's angry."

As expected, Saul's commitment wavered. "Well, if you really want."

"I'll go with you," Erin said. "You can't scare me off."

"No," Kevin snapped. He knew how Navy would react. She would yell and she would cry. She would berate whoever was there to deliver the news. She would bludgeon the messenger with her anger and grief. And Kevin deserved nothing less.

"Kevin, you're not—"

"Fuck off." Kevin stormed away toward to his car. It was bar closing time. He wanted to floor the accelerator, but he knew police would be on the watch for drunk drivers. The last thing he needed in his mood was to get pulled over.

He let himself into Jackson's building using a spare set of keys. Kevin approached the apartment with quiet steps as he tried to find the right words. *We were ambushed. I ran away.* Let Navy blame him. He blamed himself. He stopped in front of the apartment door, with its familiar nicks and scratches. Kevin's hand formed a loose fist, then hovered near the peephole. Something dripped from his chin, and he wiped his face with a sleeve. He was crying.

There was no point in delay. Kevin knocked lightly, guessing Navy would be awake. Footsteps padding to the door told him he was right. She wasn't even dressed for bed. In the corner, her work laptop screen glowed. Navy shook her head, reading the news in Kevin's face. Breath crossed her lips without sound, though her lips formed the word 'no.'

"They captured him," Kevin said. "I'm going to try, but I don't think we'll get him back." The image of the open door and Navy wavered, replaced by the swarm of soldiers pulling Jackson down. Kevin could hear Jackson's grunts punctuate the bloodthirsty cries of his attackers.

Navy's fingertips turned white as she gripped the door. Anyone else would have thought she was taking the news well. Kevin knew better. He pushed his way inside.

Her eyes were red from the effort of not crying. "Get out."

The line between grief and anger was thin. "You have things to say. Say them."

Navy's voice slammed against Kevin's chest. "You promised me!"

Kevin was expecting the fist that swung at his head. He trapped her in a loose hug. Her fists descended on his chest.

"You made me send him! You said you'd bring him back! This is your fault!"

The last line was repeated over and over as Kevin felt bruises forming. He didn't object. She was right. The least Kevin could do was carry her through to the next stage. The screen on her computer switched to her screensaver, scrolling panoramic images from her various climbing trips. He recognized the craggy outcrops and green meadows of Grayson Highlands State Park. She and Jackson had made that trip together.

"I'm sorry," Kevin whispered.

Uneven breaths shook her body. Navy didn't need him to be strong anymore. Jackson's living room blurred behind his own tears. They cried together until Navy pushed him away. The combination of salt and his exhaustion left his eyes burning.

Navy wiped her face on her sleeve before she let Kevin see her. "How long has it been since you slept?" she asked.

"Thirty-six hours." Kevin said. "I haven't been able to sleep since...."

"You shouldn't drive home right now. You can crash on the couch if you want." A mask of grief contorted Navy's face again, before she recomposed herself. "I finally convinced him to buy a new one."

Kevin didn't know if her offer was because she wanted him there, or because she could see he was dead on his feet. "If you don't mind."

Navy limply gestured at the large square ottoman. "Pillows and bedding are in there." Then she went into the bedroom and shut the door.

Chapter 18

Even knowing the risks, Navy had never really considered the possibility that Jackson wouldn't come back. If Jackson were here, he would tell her it was because she was good at dodging her emotions. He was right. If only Kevin had left when she asked him to. Navy had made a fool of herself, wailing like a goddamn princess. She had been alone before. Before Jackson, she had been alone for a long time.

She could do it again.

But then Navy looked at the bed, with Jackson's pillow and his nightstand. His clothes, waiting for his return. The top shelf with their climbing equipment: neatly coiled ropes, his-and-her harnesses, scratched helmets from their last adventure. She fell into the sheets tangled from last night's sleep and curled up as grief crashed over her again. Could Kevin hear her crying? Navy couldn't hear herself.

There was only abandonment, like a sledgehammer, pounding against her temples and emptying her lungs. Each fresh wave of emotion hurt more than the last. She wasn't just drowning; she was caught at the bottom of a whirlpool, gasping for air. Instinctively, she wished for Jackson's arms. His presence was the lifeline she reached for when she was at her worst.

But his absence was the source of her torment.

"I miss you," she whispered into the wet sheets. "I can't handle your death without you."

Exhaustion did not bring sleep. Numbly, she passed the hours. When the sky lightened, the too-bright orb of the sun pierced the horizon and pushed time forward. Navy's stomach growled, but the thought of food made her nauseous. Coffee. Coffee she could do. She rolled out of bed and carefully opened the door. Kevin might still be sleeping. Her caution wasn't out of politeness. Navy didn't want him to see her looking worse than last night.

She pulled coffee grounds from the freezer. Navy's hand shook as she measured the dark, coarse powder into the filter. It reminded her of fresh earth and burial. What would she tell Jackson's parents? His brother? Navy had only talked to them once, briefly, over the phone. Secrets had to be kept. His family thought he worked for a store sourcing handcrafted goods. There would be a story; Jackson died, perhaps, in a single-engine plane while scouting new suppliers in Zambia. An accident small enough not to make the national news, large enough there would be no body to bury.

Enough. Get through today, she told herself. The agency would, no doubt, give her orders. Just like they had ordered her to tell Min Gyu that Jackson was coming. She shoved the filter basket into the coffee machine, nearly knocking the coffee pot off the counter. So much for not waking Kevin. But he didn't stir. Navy risked a closer look. Even asleep, Kevin didn't seem relaxed. His hawk nose and lined face seemed intent on solving a problem. For all his brusqueness, Kevin was good at that.

The coffee machine hissed and sputtered, releasing an aroma like dark chocolate into the small kitchen. Memories crowded Navy's space. Slow, lazy weekend mornings spent lingering over omelets or cinnamon rolls baked from a package. Harried mornings spent tripping over each other as they rushed to work, then regretting their sharp comments. It was all over. The good and the bad. The needing and wanting and supporting and failing each other. All the things she had said that she wanted to take back, and all the things she should have said that she never did.

"Morning."

Navy dropped the empty mug she'd been holding. The ceramic broke into three pieces on the linoleum floor. Navy bumped heads with Kevin as he tried to help. "Just sit," she told him.

Kevin took a chair at the table. "I'm sorry. Was it—"

"Special?" She couldn't help the sneer in her voice. She tried again. "It was only a mug. You startled me."

"Erin wanted to come with me." Kevin rubbed his temples. "Maybe I should have let her. I'm no good at this."

One last hiss and the coffee was finished. Navy turned the machine off. "I don't want to talk."

Kevin absorbed the insult without blinking. "Work will understand that you need some time away. I'll make sure you're not bothered." He rubbed an invisible spot on the table. Then softer, "I can do that."

Navy was surprised to see two mugs sitting on the counter. She must have taken them out. Hadn't she wanted Kevin to leave?

For the first time, Navy contemplated what life in DC without Jackson would mean. Her closest friends here were Byron, Erin, and Kevin. Also Jackson's friends. They were the last living pieces of him she had left.

"You can stay for a cup," Navy told Kevin. "If you don't mind quiet."

"Sounds good to me."

Navy filled both mugs and sat one in front of Kevin. They drank in silence, as promised, though she suspected their thoughts ran in parallel. Blame and grief, and yes, anger. At the soldiers that had taken Jackson. If any North Korean soldier appeared in front of her now, Navy knew she would kill him, ethics be damned. She hoped that Jackson had taken a couple down on his way out.

Kevin's gaze crossed, but never met, hers. He was silent, as promised. The leaden air was reluctant to flow through her lungs. The discomfort was a salve, of sorts. Jackson was gone, and nothing would be okay for a long time. And that was okay.

Chapter 19

Operation Ottoman post-mortem, the meeting invite read. Erin resisted the urge to throw her laptop into the garbage. Post-mortem, indeed. Erin should have been inside that factory with her rifle, instead of scoping outside. Maybe things would have gone differently.

No, she corrected herself. Kevin was as ruthless as she was. If there'd been a way to save Jackson, Kevin would have. Erin closed her laptop more forcefully than necessary and made her way to the conference room. For the past two days, she'd been trying hard not to think too much. Certainly, Jackson wasn't the first person she knew who had died in the line of duty. But, after coming up through the ranks together and surviving for so long, Erin had become accustomed to his presence. If she had friends, Jackson would qualify as one.

Saul cleared his throat as Erin entered the room. She was late. Good. Erin didn't care if Saul was angry. Kevin glanced up, looking more tired than usual. She took a seat next to him.

According to Kevin, Navy hadn't left the apartment or answered her phone since Kevin's visit. IT said she hadn't even turned on her work laptop. Navy needed time, Erin knew. But how much time alone? It was hard to say.

There were a pair of twins she didn't recognize. The North Korean analysts Kevin had mentioned, Uri and Eli. Thankfully, the troll Peter was absent.

"What the fuck are we doing here?" Kevin asked. "You want me to read my after-action report aloud?" It was as emotional as Erin had ever seen him.

Saul shook his head. "I read it. We have a ... problem."

Erin almost laughed. "Yeah, Jackson's dead."

The lines in Saul's forehead deepened as he frowned. "I have to show you something I was hoping I wouldn't have to show you. I hope you'll understand after I explain." Saul tapped his fingers against the manila folder under his palm. "I thought this was better than using the projector. Maybe not. I guess it doesn't matter." He opened the folder and held out an 8" by 5" photograph. Erin's mind rejected what she saw at first; it was too painful.

Jackson had not gone peacefully. One eye was nearly swollen shut. Dried and fresh blood leaked from cuts on his forehead and cheeks. This was not how Erin wanted to remember him.

Erin's throat struggled to open wide enough to speak. "You said you would explain."

"We were contacted via back channels, as we had expected. Typical North Korean grandstanding bullshit. They emailed us this photo." For a split-second, Erin saw his lips curl in a snarl. "They even sent the photo to Navy."

"She can't see this," Kevin said. "Have it deleted from her account."

Saul nodded. "Already done." Saul reached across the table and turned the photo over, as if it were too hard for him to look at too. "We asked for his body and they said no, as we expected. We thought that was the end of it."

Kevin hadn't looked away from the photo, even now that it was turned over.

"And?" Erin asked.

"A second email account keeps sending us the photo, no message. Just the photo. We sent it to forensics for examination. The tech department say there's something hidden there. Using steganography. Like in the first photo Navy got."

"Another encrypted message," one of the twins said.

The image of a bloody, defeated Jackson blocked Erin's thoughts.

"And you think the message is encrypted with Navy's key, Uri," Kevin said.

"We need her to decrypt it," Uri said.

If anything, Saul looked more uncomfortable. "I hate to ask. I know you said we should leave her alone. And I would. I delayed them this long. But there's pressure from the top. I thought you two were the best ones to talk to her. She doesn't have to see the picture. She just needs to run the commands to decrypt the message."

"What's the point?" Kevin sent the stiff paper sliding back to Saul. "They think Min Gyu's asking for a second chance? And we're supposed to trust him after what happened?"

Uri tentatively leaned forward. "It could be all he's allowed to send."

A nasty look from Eli made Uri shrink back. "Or they're mocking us. North Korean fucking mind games."

"I'm with him," Erin said. "They're letting him send email in between torture sessions? Right."

Saul gingerly put the picture back in his folder. "You know how it is. Management wants to see if the operation can be salvaged. No stone unturned. All that."

Erin respected Saul for his honesty, but not enough to help. "We're not going to bother Navy about some bullshit errand just because the suits want us to." She looked at Kevin for support.

Instead, she saw Kevin's body frozen in a mix of disgust and resignation. "What Saul means to say is we have to ask Navy to decrypt the message or they'll send someone else."

Saul's bowed head affirmed Kevin's statement.

"Thanks for trying, anyway," Kevin said flatly. "We'll go to Navy's apartment now. Have the file sent to my email."

Even having known Kevin for ten years, Erin couldn't tell if Kevin was really thankful or just rubbing salt in the wound. She scrambled to follow Kevin.

Kevin slammed the car into gear. Mid-morning traffic was light, and he took full advantage of the open highway. With any other driver, the risks he was taking would have frightened Erin. They arrived at Jackson's apartment twenty minutes later.

"She's going to hate us for this," Erin said.

"Maybe," Kevin said.

Erin counted the people she might consider friends. Without Jackson, there were three left and Navy was one of them.

Kevin shut the car off and sighed. "I can't have her lashing out at some random twerp who shows up demanding she decrypt the message. Maybe she'll forgive me, maybe she won't. But if we don't do this, she'll be out of a job on top of everything else. You don't have to come with me."

"No, I'm coming." The words surprised Erin. Yes, Navy would be angry with her. But being angry and alone would be worse. At least, that's what Erin hoped.

Erin smiled at the old woman in the elevator, just home from the store with her groceries in a wire cart. The woman got off on Navy's floor, then turned down the hallway. Neither Kevin nor Erin moved. When the door was about to shut, Erin stuck a foot out. "It's not going to get any easier if we wait."

Kevin nodded. "Yeah, I know."

They could hear the TV behind Navy's door. She didn't answer on the first knock or the second. Kevin looked at the keys in his hand, weighing a decision.

Erin understood. Letting themselves in if Navy was willfully ignoring them was a violation.

One more round of knocking went unanswered. Kevin rubbed his forehead, then addressed the door. "It's me, Navy. And Erin. We need to talk."

The TV volume got louder.

"I have keys," Kevin said. "If you don't let us in."

Still nothing.

Erin grabbed the keys and opened the door. The only light in the room was a flickering TV screen. Some action movie with Jet Li. Erin's eyes had trouble identifying the unmoving lump on the couch piled with blankets as Navy.

The voice that emerged from the hollow-eyed face was as strong as ever. "I told you I didn't want to talk," Navy said.

Erin found Navy's laptop and sat on the carpet next to the couch. Erin was stinging from guilt from the state Navy was in. They had left Navy alone for too long, and now they had to talk business. Navy's eyes were red and her face was drawn. The only evidence of activity in the kitchen was a half-empty glass of water.

"There's another message, Navy. The North Koreans have been sending it to us since he was captured," Erin said. "The suits aren't willing to admit the operation was a failure, and they want you to decrypt it."

Navy blinked and settled into her blankets. "Good for them."

"I've seen you do this a hundred times now. Just unlock your screen, and I'll set it up so all you have to do is type the passphrase for your key," Kevin said.

Erin hoped grief would smother Navy's natural curiosity, just for a little longer.

"There's another image?" Navy asked. The pile of blankets shifted.

Kevin sighed. "You don't want to see it, trust me."

Navy's eyes narrowed as she untangled herself from her covers and sat up. "No deal. If I'm going to decrypt the message, you're going to show me the image."

What did Navy think she was going to see? Or did Navy think she deserved the pain? "Navy, it's bad. It's Jackson . . . after . . ." *After they tortured him.* Erin couldn't say the words aloud.

Navy grabbed her laptop and unlocked it, then handed it back to Kevin. "The image. Now."

Kevin and Erin shared a long look. They both had scar tissue that blunted the impact of seeing their good friend brutally defeated. The combination of Navy's guilt and Jackson's painful ending might put Navy on the couch for another month.

Kevin frowned and typed for a minute. Erin saw him pulling up his email, downloading the photo, then minimizing the window. Kevin held onto the laptop for a long minute.

"It won't help you to see it, Navy," Kevin said. "But if you want to look, go ahead and open it."

Navy snatched the laptop and opened the image. For a microsecond, she had the same expression Kevin had on first seeing it. Then Navy almost seemed cheered.

"Why didn't you show me this earlier?" Navy demanded.

Why would I do that to you? "You know why we didn't show you," Erin said finally.

Navy shook her head excitedly and turned the screen around. She had blown up the image to highlight a cluster of red pixels in the lower left-hand corner. Kevin visibly flinched. "It's photoshopped," Navy said. "It's a fake. This is the same signature Min Gyu put on the original photo."

"A fake?" Erin asked.

"He's not dead." Navy gripped the sides of her laptop, nearly smiling. "Don't you get it? Min Gyu used photoshop to fake his death."

"Navy—" Erin said.

"I'll show you." Navy typed furiously, then triumphantly displayed a message on the screen.

```
Jackson is alive. I didn't betray you, I
swear. I was being watched. Someone in
State Security guessed at my plans. He
interrupted the rescue because he wants to
defect. His name is Ryu Yung Bo, or Yung
Bo Ryu as you would say in the West. He is
a Major General. Yung Bo supervised
Jackson's interrogation so he could fake
your partner's death. Yung Bo said I
should doctor the photo to make Jackson's
injuries look worse so everyone would
believe it. I am sorry you had to see this
photo, but it was the only way I could get
the message past our censors. Yung Bo is
hiding us. He will let Jackson and I go,
if you take him too. Please advise. I have
setup a new email address and key. The old
email is compromised. Hurry.
```

It was good news. Mostly.

"We can get him back." Navy studied both their faces, frustration clearly showing on hers. "What's wrong? You think Min Gyu is lying?"

Kevin frowned. "Not exactly."

"A Major General in State Security has resources at his disposal. Money, power, a good excuse to travel. South Korea would love to shelter him in return for everything in his head." Erin said. She hoped she could temper Navy's hopes. "He could have quietly approached Min Gyu and asked to be included or tried to defect on his own. But instead, Yung Bo mobilizes a force of sixty men, captures an American agent, and fakes the agent's death."

Kevin pressed his lips together into a thin line. "Yung Bo's holding hostages. He can't get out on his own, and he doesn't think we'll take him by himself."

Anger replaced Navy's relief. "I'll go get Jackson if no one else will."

Erin risked touching Navy's arm. The instinct to comfort was new to her. "We'll get him," she promised. And she meant it. Officially or unofficially. "But it's going to be complicated. Suits don't like complicated."

Chapter 20

Min Gyu had never been in a nicer place, and he had never felt more like a prisoner. Day or night was irrelevant; his room had no windows. The bed was comfortable, at least. A thick pillowtop mattress with silk sheets and a goose down duvet. The bathroom included both a Jacuzzi tub and a couples' shower. Min Gyu had heard stories of such places, dangled in front of him by his uncle in the hopes that Min Gyu would pursue jobs with more political power.

By Min Gyu's guess, they were in one of the infamous Kim mansions. Kim Il Sung had begun the tradition of building various vacation houses, and both Kims since had continued. Because of satellite photography, the mansions were never completely dark. There were a couple hundred or so lucky people whose job was to wander around and inhabit these places so the CIA would never know for sure where Kim Jong Eun was. Min Gyu had heard their footsteps and voices in the hallway. Min Gyu was trapped in a luxurious Potemkin village.

Min Gyu could have walked out and taken his chances; the room wasn't locked. What kept him from trying to escape was the occupant of the large walk-in closet next to the bathroom. The American. Jackson was too weak to move. The hour changed on the clock from 11:59 to 12:00. Noon or midnight? Min Gyu had to think. He hadn't seen the afternoon news yet. Noon. Time to see to the patient.

Or he could wait until the next propaganda break in the movie he was watching. *No, stop stalling.* Jackson's injuries were Min Gyu's fault.

Min Gyu picked up the tray holding food and medicine. As he had three times a day for the last two days, he knocked gently on the door to announce his presence, then pushed it open. The American lifted himself up on his elbows then sank back down with a grimace.

"Keep still," Min Gyu cautioned as he forced a smile. "Doctor's orders."

The comment hung in the air like a bad smell. Yung Bo's orders, really. And neither of them trusted the major general.

Min Gyu opened the bottle of water and held up a small plastic cup of pills. "Antibiotics and pain killers." Yung Bo could have left the bottles of pills in the room, instead of dispensing them one day at a time. Perhaps Yung Bo was afraid one of them would commit suicide with the painkillers. Or he wanted to keep them dependent.

Jackson lifted his head so Min Gyu could give him water. Jackson swallowed the pills with effort. "Day three?" he asked.

Min Gyu nodded.

"No word?"

"Eat. She'll contact us soon. I'm sure of it."

Min Gyu wasn't sure at all. It couldn't have been easy for Navy to see the picture Yung Bo had forced him to make. She might not have noticed Min Gyu's signature in the corner. Yung Bo insisted the picture had to be gruesome to be realistic. Min Gyu suspected the major general liked the idea of torturing Navy by proxy.

Just like Yung Bo enjoyed sending food that required chewing, when it was obviously painful for Jackson to do so. Min Gyu ripped off a small piece of the sandwich, remembering how much it had hurt for Jackson just to swallow. "Okay if I try something?"

Jackson nodded slightly.

Min Gyu put the square of sandwich in one of the empty pill cups and poured water over it. The effect wasn't appetizing. But it would be easier to chew. The soggy bread dripped brown when he held it up. "Don't look too closely," Min Gyu said.

What might have been a smile crinkled the corners of Jackson's eyes. "I've had worse."

Min Gyu saw the grimace when the American's jaw moved, even slightly. Better perhaps, but still not easy.

When half the sandwich was gone, Jackson held up a hand and lowered himself to rest. "A break."

Min Gyu looked anywhere but at the man he had nearly killed. A pasty with red sequins and a silver tassel was stuck in the corner of the closet. One of the Corps girls had been here performing for the occupant of the room. Not for the exalted leader himself—the room wasn't opulent enough for that. But perhaps a general, or even Min Gyu's uncle. A girl whose parents might have welcomed her status as a chosen one, because it meant a position of relative safety. Sometimes Min Gyu thought the combined misery of his country would smother him.

Jackson cleared his throat. He had pushed himself up again, ready to eat. "You're not a bad person."

Yes, I am. "I believed once."

"You were taught to."

Min Gyu shook his head. "You don't understand. My father taught me the truth." Min Gyu prepared another mouthful of food. The bread soaked up the water like a sponge, then wilted and softened. "How do you think I learned my trade? My father smuggled in the parts of a computer the CIA gave him, and we built it together. While he typed the reports, we practiced our English. For when we escaped. When the computer broke, we fixed it together. There were others we weren't supposed to know about. But sometimes we would meet, by accident. My father told me how to contact them using messages on the tapes. In case."

The American took the bite of food with more energy than the last. A good sign.

"After my parents disappeared, my uncle showed up to adopt me. I was scared. I had lost everything." Min Gyu remembered coming home to find his mother gone. Normally, his mother had rice cooking and the table set. Min Gyu had taken a chair at the bare table in his empty house. He sat there for hours, hoping this wasn't the moment his parents had been worried about. But then Min Gyu's uncle had showed up with his scheming fake sadness and said there'd been an accident.

"You were vulnerable," Jackson said.

"You won't forgive me when I finish the story." Min Gyu fed Jackson again. The mush left a coating on Min Gyu's hands. He wiped them on his pant legs. "My uncle told me he knew about what my parents had been doing. My uncle was very calculating. He introduced me to his friends and their children. They were all happy. They were all privileged, but I didn't know that at the time. My uncle told me that my father had lied about how bad the regime was." Min Gyu could feel his fingernails digging into his own thighs. "Privately, he told me that my parents had disgraced the family name. My uncle said I was lucky that he could speak for me, that I would have a chance to bring honor to our family."

Jackson looked confused. "The government knew your father was an agent, and you were spared?"

Another mouthful of food. Another silent moment that begged for confession. "My uncle lied," Min Gyu said. "Only he knew what my parents had done. But my uncle needed me. For his promotion."

Jackson's bloodshot eyes widened. Jackson had guessed the end of Min Gyu's story.

"My uncle saved the computer and some of the tapes. He said if I—" The freshness of the image surprised Min Gyu. That ambush had happened nearly twenty years ago. And yet, he could still see the anguished man's face. A family friend tackled and ambushed, like Jackson had been. Gam Iseul. The worst part was what Iseul hadn't done. As the soldiers dragged him away, Iseul hadn't called Min Gyu a diseased body or the son of a whore. Iseul had simply wilted into his captors' arms. As if he had expected Min Gyu would fail to live up to his father's memory. To this day, Min Gyu wondered why Iseul had come, what he had promised Min Gyu's father.

"You turned someone in," Jackson said.

"I murdered a friend," Min Gyu said.

Jackson's hard eyes weren't forgiving. Min Gyu was glad.

"If we can get out of here, you can cut the heart out of a dictatorship," Jackson said.

"It's not enough."

"It's never enough." Jackson's faraway eyes were reliving his own memories. "But it's something."

"Eat," Min Gyu told him. And Jackson did.

152

Chapter 21

Navy steered the car around a cluster of orange cones behind a utility truck. A woman in a white hardhat was pulling fiber cable from a spool nearly as big as Navy's car. Lucky neighborhood, Navy thought. "Turn left on Grove Avenue," her GPS announced politely.

Kevin, sitting in the passenger seat, cleared his throat. "Mind telling me where we're going?"

"You'll see," Navy said. It had been a week since Jackson's capture. Five days since she had learned he was alive. And nobody was giving her answers.

Grove Avenue, and the neighborhood, was everything she expected. Navy could write a random word generator that would have named half the streets in these new housing developments. Glens, dales, forests, lakes, and laurels—all the things being replaced by the prefabricated mansions.

Navy felt bad for annoying Kevin. But not too bad, because Kevin hadn't asked for her help. She was going to help anyway.

She pulled into the large parking lot outside Glenview Medical Clinic. The siding on the clinic matched the houses on the next block. When Navy passed the empty parking spot right in front of the door, Kevin raised his eyebrows. When she patiently began to search each row, Kevin looked annoyed again.

"I know we're not here for my health," Kevin said.

Navy ignored him. Could be that blue sedan right there. Navy would know when she could see the plates. Yep, she'd found it. Both spots next to the sedan were taken. She parked in front of it and checked her watch. Just in time.

Now for the final piece, the small black box she had built and stored in the glove compartment.

"Patience. You'll see why we're here in a minute."

"Patience isn't my strong suit," Kevin said.

Navy flicked a switch on the black box. Exactly as she'd planned, a tall man with a ponytail appeared outside the front door of the clinic. When Kevin noticed Saul approaching them, Kevin shook his head. "I thought I was supposed to be the unreasonable one."

Navy smiled. "I learned from the best."

Saul didn't see them at first. He pushed a button on his remote to open the car, then looked confused when the door didn't unlock. Time to make her appearance. Navy opened her door and Kevin reluctantly followed.

"What the—" Saul held up his remote. "Do you have something to do with this?"

It was always a nice surprise when her toys worked as well as she hoped. She hadn't had much time to test. "Maybe you should try the physical key?" Navy said.

Saul turned the key in the lock, but immediately there was a click as the door locked again.

"Huh. Guess you're locked out," Navy said. "Until I get some answers."

"A little help?" Saul asked Kevin.

Kevin was doing his best to hide a smile. "Clearly, I'm not the one in charge here."

"Speaking of," Saul said. "How did you know I'd be here? Have you hacked my phone?"

"Nothing that complicated," Navy said. "I was in your email, remember? They sent you an appointment reminder."

Saul's glare would have intimidated Navy two weeks ago. "You've violated at least a dozen different laws here, not to mention the code of conduct," Saul said.

"I don't care." A flash of anger sharpened Navy's next words. "I spend two days thinking my boyfriend is dead because you didn't keep me in the loop. I had to tell you, the people who are supposed to know things, that he's alive and *we can rescue him* and now I can't seem to find both of you in the office at the same time. Ever."

"It's complicated," Saul said.

Navy crossed her arms. "Try me."

"Would you please tell her to be reasonable?" Saul asked Kevin.

A bitter smile twisted Kevin's lips. "No, I want to hear this excuse again. Explain to me why we haven't rescued Jackson."

Saul glanced around. "This really isn't the place."

Navy checked her watch. "Isn't your daughter's soccer tournament in ten minutes? It's so nice that she's almost made it to finals."

Saul threw up his hands. "You understand you only get to pull this stunt with me exactly once."

"I promise I won't ever work with you again."

Kevin nudged her. He was telling her to be careful.

Saul looked around to make sure the parking lot was empty of people. "We have directors from multiple agencies and several senators involved at this point. They're nervous that maybe Min Gyu is lying to us and that he knew Jackson would be captured. Or Yung Bo is lying to us about letting Jackson and Min Gyu go. Yung Bo Ryu has approached us before seeking asylum. We don't trust him. Even if Yung Bo's not lying, there's still the problem of what to do with him. South Korea says he's not defecting for ideological reasons. It's party politics. His allies are weakening. Our profilers tell us he's an amoral opportunist. He'll say whatever he thinks we want to hear, then he'll work for whomever pays him the most." Saul leaned forward, clearly angry now. "The delay is because I've been calling any other country that might take Yung Bo. The South Koreans don't trust him any more than we do. The Chinese don't want to disturb their mining contracts. The Russians don't care about North Korea anymore. I'm telling you, I've called everyone. No one wants him. And there's no political appetite for detaining Yung Bo indefinitely without a trial. And there can't be a trial because then we would have to come up with a story for how Yung Bo made it to the United States."

"I can solve that problem for you," Kevin said.

His tone made Navy go cold. Kevin meant rescuing Yung Bo just to kill him.

"And I've told you, this operation is now too high profile for us to get away with that. They're worried about a leak exposing the U.S. government's targeted assassination of a refugee seeking asylum." Saul looked at Navy. "You know, kind of like what you did."

Only the possibility of Jackson's rescue kept Navy from going for Saul's throat. Meditation breaths, she told herself. "You're a smart asshole. I'm sure you can think of something."

"You think I don't want this operation to work!" Saul looked around to make sure no one had heard his outburst. "I have tried everything I can think of. I have no other options."

Navy leaned against her car. This was the end of her plan. She had figured the delay was simple bureaucracy. Would Jackson agree with Kevin's plan to assassinate Yung Bo? Did Navy agree with Kevin's plan? Did it matter? Keeping Saul locked out of his car wasn't going to get Jackson rescued.

"You owed me an explanation," Navy said. "I guess I have one now." She reached into her car to turn off the black box that was continually sending the signal to relock Saul's car. "Your key should work."

Saul hesitated before getting into the driver's seat. "I'm sorry, Navy. Really, I am."

Navy blinked away tears as she watched Saul drive away. She was losing Jackson all over again.

"Give me the keys," Kevin said. "I'll drive you home."

"If you want to help," Navy said, "stop treating me like a child."

Chapter 22

Kevin figured it was only fair to ambush Saul at the concessions stand at his daughter's soccer game. After all, Saul had disturbed Kevin's time with Irving.

By the looks of the line, the concession bar would sell out. Navy hadn't just threatened to make him late for a soccer game. This was a tournament to qualify for the finals next week. And Saul, who was a good twenty yards from the front of the concession line, would have plenty of time to talk to Kevin.

Saul's eyes narrowed when Kevin slipped into line next to him. "Twice in one day. Where's your sidekick?"

Kevin had left Navy, red-eyed, at the apartment she shared with Jackson. "Stabbing pins into voodoo dolls of you, I imagine."

"Well, that explains the headache I got when I saw you."

A group of teenagers in front of Saul glanced up from their phones. Kevin put on a genial expression to keep them disinterested. "I'm here to make a deal."

"Is it different than the one you offered the committee?"

Assassinating Yung Bo after rescuing Jackson and Min Gyu hadn't gone over well, even though Kevin had been careful about his audience. Jackson's high profile "death" meant senators and multiple agency directors were involved now. Kevin would never admit it, but Saul wasn't wrong. Yung Bo couldn't disappear because of the United States government. At least, not in a way that was traceable to them. "Not a deal with the committee. A deal with you. Think of what a success like this could mean for your career."

Saul's interest was evidenced only by a slight movement in his eyebrows.

In a public place, Kevin had to choose his words carefully. "Tell everyone you have an offer for a home. I'll make sure you never have to follow through."

"That doesn't sound all that different."

Kevin fought to keep the edge from his voice. "A deal between us. No one else knows."

"Not even your sidekick?"

"Especially not her."

"What if it looks like our fault?"

"It won't."

"And if someone finds out?"

"Say you didn't know. Blame me. Say I did it for revenge."

Saul's hard eyes flickered to something resembling sympathy. "You'll be forced out. They may even prosecute you."

"I know."

"Then I guess the only question is if you're as good as you think you are."

Cheers and clapping erupted behind them. Someone yelled "Gooooooooal!" The crowd got louder as a group of girls streamed onto the field to hug their teammates.

Kevin took advantage of the noise and distraction to make his words more direct. "My job is to protect men like Jackson from men like you. And I'm *very* good at it."

Saul's reply was nearly a whisper. The edge in his voice cut through the continuing celebration. "I'm exactly the man you think I am. If someone finds out, I will crucify you."

"We understand each other then. Make your preparations. I want wheels up in twenty-four hours. And you'll tell Navy the good news."

"Or else she'll figure out we made a deal."

Kevin didn't bother to reply. They had lost the cover of the crowd noise anyway. He was glad he hadn't outlined to the committee exactly how Yung Bo would die. They had cut him off before he had a chance. His original plan would work just fine.

Chapter 25

Jackson and Min Gyu had been trapped in the opulent mansion for seven days now. From the closet that was his recovery room, Jackson recognized the theme song of the show Min Gyu always watched in the morning. The music swelled into yet another patriotic anthem, no doubt singing the praises of the Great Leader. If Jackson had asked, Min Gyu would have moved him into the large room. Jackson preferred the closet. He spent most of his hours sleeping. He suspected the pain medication Yung Bo had provided was an opioid. The white pills made Jackson feel like he was floating above the pain in his swollen gums and the tender, healing scabs that covered his body. Infrequently, he heard sounds that might have been from the hallway. Jackson's dulled senses left him uncomfortably vulnerable, but without the meds he was unable to sleep.

Without sleep he could not heal. Without healing, he could not escape.

Seven days in a dark closet had given Jackson a lot of time to think. The only explanation for Yung Bo's convoluted scheme was desperation. A man with Yung Bo's resources should be able to leave the country on trips for official state business. A man with Yung Bo's knowledge would be a valuable asset to half a dozen countries, if they trusted him. Doubtless, Yung Bo had sought asylum before and been turned away.

Jackson and Min Gyu weren't just prisoners, they were hostages.

A door opened and closed, perhaps on the television, perhaps in the room. Jackson struggled to focus. It could be Yung Bo delivering medication, as he did every day. But something was different today. Yes, someone was in the room, speaking to Min Gyu. It wasn't just the television. Something heavy and solid was set on a table. The sweeping music of the show faded, and in the relative quiet Jackson heard keys clicking. Someone was typing. A message had arrived.

Yung Bo sounded as if he were dictating something to Min Gyu. A response? Jackson wondered how it was possible. He doubted Yung Bo would follow through on the deal and let Jackson and Min Gyu go. Jackson heard Yung Bo leave. He waited for Min Gyu to deliver the news, but the closet doors did not open. Various bruises and cuts protested as Jackson pushed himself up and off his cot. He hobbled unsteadily in the semi-darkness of his cocoon, then swung the double doors of the closet open.

Min Gyu sat on the edge of the bed, grinning and crying at the same time. "We are leaving tonight. In twelve hours, you are going home."

The nightmare wouldn't end that easily. Jackson eased himself into a sitting position on the bed. "How?"

"A boat will pick us up ten miles off the coast. We just sent them the coordinates."

Jackson did some calculations in his head, none of which made him feel any better. If Yung Bo had access to a boat, they'd be on it already. "That's a long way to travel without a way to get there."

Min Gyu's answer was a smile. "Kim Jong Il was a great fan of James Bond movies."

Chapter 26

The barbed wire fence surrounding the Army base was the least of Navy's worries. She leaned over the steering wheel and eyed the gate around the corner. Beyond the guards, a plane was busy being prepared for takeoff. If Jackson were beside her, he would say that she was being foolhardy and reckless. But Jackson wasn't. And that's why Navy was here.

Navy pressed down on the accelerator before she could change her mind. A young man in uniform holding a clipboard walked up to her window.

"This facility is for authorized personnel only, ma'am."

She tapped the bright red baseball cap on the passenger seat, branded with a golden "M." The short-sleeved polo shirt she wore had the same logo. "I'm here to fill in at the food court. The manager called because they're shorthanded."

The guard frowned. "Do you have photo ID?"

Navy pulled her driver's license out of her wallet. Despite the news coverage three years ago, she was now relatively unknown. The world had moved on to other scandals.

"I meant the access card you use to get on base. Not your license."

"I don't usually work at this location." She looked down, as if she were upset, and fidgeted with her hands. "I'm just filling in, I mean, this is my first time. And it took me a while to find the place. I got lost, and now I'm going to be late."

The best hacks were the simplest hacks. And social engineering on a base this big, with this many people coming and going, was almost too easy. Navy could see from his worried expression that the guard was sympathetic. He gestured to a parking area near a cluster of drab buildings.

"Go straight to the food court. It's up there on the left."

Navy smiled with the proper humility and gratefulness. "Thank you so much."

After she parked, she zipped up her coat to hide the bright red shirt and clipped a blank white plastic badge to her belt. The edge of the badge just peeked out under the jacket. Enough to make someone who had other things to do assume she was authorized. Then the hardest part was walking like she knew where she was going. Because she didn't.

The airfield was visible from the entrance. Finding the hangar would be more difficult. Erin and Kevin would have been escorted to the correct hangar on arrival, since their names were on the list. Navy would have to wander, without looking like she was wandering.

The first hangar was nearly empty, except for a few men in uniform loading supplies. Navy kept her head down and walked, she hoped, not too fast and not too slow. Just as she was about to peek into the second hangar, a pair of tan boots stepped into her path. The man wearing them looked decidedly less friendly than the guard at the gate. And larger. A shock of red hair surrounded a freckled face and narrowed green eyes.

"I'll need to see your base ID, ma'am." His southern drawl didn't soften the command. "This is a restricted area."

Being a fast-food worker wouldn't buy her much here. A reservist who'd lost her uniform, perhaps. No, best to stick closer to the truth. "I'm a CIA tech." Navy knew there was a volunteer list at the CIA for techs needed on combat missions.

The man smiled coldly. "Are you now. Let's see your ID."

Reluctantly, Navy pulled out her CIA ID card. Might as well go for broke. "I'm here for Operation Ottoman. Can you direct me?"

His hand closed around her forearm and yanked her into the hangar. "You're coming with me. Commander, we have a problem."

The man who appeared from behind the plane had gray eyes that matched the streaks of gray in his hair. "They said you were resourceful."

"Commander?" asked the man holding Navy's arm.

"Ozark, meet Jackson's girlfriend, Navy Trent. Navy Trent, meet my weapons officer, Ozark. I'm Garrett, the commander in charge of this mission."

Ozark released her arm, and she felt blood flowing again. Navy swallowed. "Nice to meet you, Ozark."

At the sound of her voice, Kevin popped out from behind a pallet of supplies. He was not happy to see her.

"Navy, what are you doing here?"

"Going with you." She hoped she sounded confident.

"The hell you are." Kevin turned to the commander. "Have her escorted off base. And held until we take off."

Garrett studied Navy for a minute. Navy wondered if he'd read her file. "I can be useful somehow. Or I can just wait at Camp Red Cloud until you get Jackson. I just can't—" Navy recomposed herself. Then to Kevin, "I won't sit here and wait. Not again. You needed my help to get this far, remember?"

Kevin's scowl didn't soften. "You're not even remotely qualified for a mission like this, Navy."

"I can fight, and I can shoot. You know that."

Kevin pointed at the row of large green bags lined up next to the plane. "Tell me what those are."

Navy didn't like where this was going. "Backpacks?"

Ozark laughed.

165

"They're parachutes," Kevin said. "Have you done a HALO jump before? At night? Over water? Into hostile territory?"

Navy had known trying to talk her way onto Jackson's rescue mission wasn't a good idea. Hearing it explained to her in front of an audience stung anyway. Erin was in the corner, packing weapons into a crate. And more men in uniform she hadn't noticed before were loading gear onto the plane. The rest of Ozark's unit, Navy guessed. They were all looking at her with the same expression, like Navy was a kid who had crashed a grownup party.

"I'll make you a deal," Kevin said. "Leave right now and I won't tell CIA security that you hacked into company files above your clearance level to get the details of our mission."

Commander Garrett was looking at Navy as if he were curious about something. He held open a rugged black case the size of a briefcase, but thicker. Nestled securely inside was a drone with four rotors and a black box with a large display. "You ever used one of these before?" the commander asked Navy.

Navy had, briefly. And there was a manual neatly stowed next to the device. "Sure."

Kevin turned to the commander. "You can't be serious."

"We were supposed to have an NSA tech with us to operate this ... sniffer thingy," Garrett said. "But it's been a bad flu season, so everyone's short-staffed. The tech backed out at the last minute. Headquarters won't green-light the mission without a tech to operate the drone."

"Rescuing Jackson isn't enough of a reason to go," Kevin said. To the group or to himself, Navy didn't know. Someone who didn't know Kevin as well as Navy did, might think he was calm.

The commander didn't look much happier. "There's a military academy in Hamhung, near the rendezvous point. They want to test their toy. It's supposed to record calls on North Korea's cell phone network."

"A stingray," Navy said. She had never seen one so small. Navy stepped forward and lifted the drone, forgetting it was held by the commander. But when she looked up, he only lifted an eyebrow. The drone was beautiful in its deviousness. No larger than a shoebox. "The engineering it took to make it this small..." Navy tested its weight with one finger. "They must have their own milling machine."

The commander grinned. "How about this deal? Come with us and make this toy work, and we'll pretend I don't know how you got here."

Navy raised her chin and stared down Kevin. "I like the commander's deal better."

Kevin's lips pressed thin. "Commander—"

For the first time, the commander's expression betrayed anger. "My mission, my rules. You want us to rescue your man? We need her. She'll tandem with Ozark."

The glare Kevin leveled at Navy made her step back.

"Jackson asked me to protect you. If you die and he comes back, he'll never forgive himself. Or me," Kevin said.

"He's not here." Unwelcome tears pricked at Navy's eyes. "I don't care what he wants."

Erin stepped between them and steered Navy toward the belly of the plane. "I'll show you where first class is."

"First, I think you'll be needing this." The commander gave Navy the manual for the drone. "You have twelve hours to become an expert."

She avoided Kevin's eyes and followed Erin onto the plane. Hard metal benches were bolted to the sides. The seat backs were green nets made of what looked like seatbelts sewn together.

Behind her, the Green Berets were loading plastic crates, like the one Erin had been packing, as well as the parachutes Navy had mistaken for backpacks and larger packs she could barely have put her arms around. The large packs were ringed with canvas straps sewn down in places to form loops. Carabiners dangled from the loops.

This was not Navy's world. She fumbled with the seat belt and forced herself to focus on the manual. The type was small and hastily formatted. The author was clearly more of a technician than writer. Navy blinked and read the page again. A forked version of Dronecode. Linux. The operating system she'd been playing with since college. This, at least, she knew.

The engines rumbled, and she felt the plane move.

I shouldn't be here. I have to be here.

Navy kept her head down and turned another page. The takeoff was bumpy, and her stomach squirmed. On a commercial flight, the captain might have made an announcement to reassure the passengers. Here, she was the only one who seemed nervous. And the only sound was the engine just behind her, somehow whining and growling at the same time.

A jolt knocked the book from her hands. Navy caught it before it fell, unconsciously checking if Kevin had seen her fumble. But Kevin was focused on something else. Navy had seen him angry before, many times. Impatient, most of the time. But she'd never seen him sad. Like he'd lost confidence in himself.

If the engines weren't so loud, or if she believed it herself, she would have told him everything was going to be okay.

Chapter 27

Pain. Jackson was glad he'd flushed all that day's pain medication down the toilet. Otherwise, he might have changed his mind. Without the pills, Jackson was coordinated and awake. But aching. And every ache reminded him of the variety of gleaming, metallic implements he'd been tortured with.

In just a few minutes, Yung Bo should arrive to lead Min Gyu and Jackson out of captivity. Probably. If Yung Bo meant to keep his promise and get his hostages safely to the extraction point. Jackson was very aware he was trusting his life to the man who carved him up with a scalpel not that many days ago.

The blue numerals on the alarm clock ticked up one more minute. 9:59 p.m. Min Gyu sat next to Jackson on the bed, staring at the door. Yung Bo was due to arrive any minute. He should have arrived already.

"What if they found out?" Min Gyu asked. "What if he's not coming?"

"Give him five more minutes." Jackson had learned a long time ago that cataloguing all possible disasters was a good way to panic.

"And if he doesn't come for us?" Min Gyu sprung off the bed. "What do we do then?"

Jackson wasn't sure. Yung Bo had set their prison up well. There wasn't much in the room that was useful as a weapon, especially in Jackson's weakened state. He had no idea what kind of security they would face beyond the door. "I've gotten out of worse," Jackson lied.

Min Gyu paced and watched the clock.

Even the slight rustle of Min Gyu's shoes against the carpet scraped at Jackson's nerves. It was sensory overload, he told himself. For a week, Jackson had spent most of his hours sleeping in the dark, with his senses dulled by the opiates in his bloodstream. His brain would adjust.

Min Gyu's arms began to flap in time with his steps. "He's not—"

The door opened. For the first time, Jackson was glad to see Yung Bo. The major general was in full uniform and carried only a small satchel. A gun was holstered at his waist. "All of the guests have retired to their rooms for the night's entertainment," Yung Bo said quietly. "It is safe for us to move now."

Jackson hid a wince as he stood. He didn't want Yung Bo to see he was still in pain. Min Gyu was already in the hallway. Even the dim hallway seemed spacious to Jackson, after so long cooped up in one room. Soft lights were spaced evenly at the height of his shoulders. Automatically, his tactical mind multiplied the number of lights by the spacing between them to estimate the length of the hallway. Fifty feet on either side of them, at least. Each foot was more time an attacker would have to spot them.

"Guests first." Yung Bo pointed toward the left.

Jackson would have done the same thing if he were in the bastard's place. As long as Yung Bo walked behind them, there was no way for Jackson to get the upper hand. Gold metallic designs on the red wallpaper winked at him as they passed. Jackson listened carefully to the cadence of the general's steps and for the whisper of metal sliding against the leather of a gun holster.

Intelligence was a betting game. Jackson had to think like his opponent. The kidnapping had been necessary to secure the deal for the general's freedom. But getting three people out was harder than escaping alone. The general had proven he was willing to take risks to earn his freedom; Yung Bo might be willing to risk showing up by himself. The worse the Americans could do was kill him. With the right preparations, he could hijack the escape boat.

Assets had taken advantage of their rescuers before.

The endless hallway finally turned a corner and opened into a large room clearly designed for entertaining. A wet bar stood diagonally in one corner, in front of shelves lined with bottles of liquor from around the world. What was missing was an exit.

Jackson spun to attack, but his lunge was stopped by the weapon Yung Bo was already pointing at him.

"Tsk, tsk," Yung Bo said. "I told you we were going to use our Supreme Leader's secret escape route. Did you think it would be clearly marked?"

Min Gyu's hands shook as he looked between Jackson and Yung Bo. "A-are you going to kill us?"

"Try the gin," Yung Bo said. "It's Nolet's Reserve."

Min Gyu didn't move.

A moment of distraction might be enough for Jackson to get the gun. "What kind of sick game is this?"

Yung Bo glanced behind him, but the gun never wavered. "Pull on the bottle of gin. Quickly, please."

Min Gyu was still frozen, so Jackson stepped toward the shelf.

"Not the soldier," Yung Bo said. "Min Gyu."

Finally, Min Gyu obeyed. Hesitantly, he touched the neck of the black bottle and pulled. The cabinet swung open to reveal a room with concrete walls.

James Bond, indeed, Jackson thought. He looked at Yung Bo for permission to move. The general's smug smile made Jackson want to kill the bastard. Not for the first time tonight, and probably not the last.

"After you," Yung Bo said.

The back of the cabinet was concrete as well. For protection from small arms, most likely. It took both Min Gyu and Jackson to push the cabinet shut.

The room was empty except for an elevator. There was no choice for up or down, just one button.

Not that surprising, Jackson thought as he pushed the button on the wall. The elevator only had one purpose. Jackson stepped into the elevator, then grabbed Min Gyu's arm and pulled him in.

Yung Bo kept the gun trained on his captives as he followed.

There was no display to tell them what floor they were on, or how many floors had passed as they descended. Jackson found himself wondering if the technician who had installed the elevator, and the engineer who had designed the escape route, had been killed like the men who hid the Pharoah's treasure.

Bright lights flickered on automatically as they stepped into a dank room. A few feet away, water lapped at the edge of a platform.

"You have to be kidding me." Jackson was staring at what looked like a set of underwater Ironman suits made for the shortest superheroes ever. They were mounted on the wall in glass cases, like every comic book superhero lair required. A small propeller was attached to each limb. Even if the dubious North Korean engineering worked, Jackson would never fit inside those suits.

"We're leaving in *those*?" Min Gyu asked.

Yung Bo shook his head. "Those are only prototypes. The Supreme Leader decided on a personal submarine."

Jackson looked around the room. There was no submarine, and no place to hide one. And no way to reach Yung Bo without getting shot in the process.

"You really don't believe me." Yung Bo seemed offended. "The submarine isn't done yet. That's why no one's paying attention to this exit right now. Open the crate against the wall. The biggest one."

Jackson felt for the clasps along the edge, coating his fingers with grime in the process. One, two, three clasps. Snap, snap, snap. His fingernails, still bloody underneath, burned. But he didn't care. Inside the crate were drysuits, tanks, and driver propulsion vehicles.

They might just make it out of this prison.

Except . . . the drysuit on top looked much newer and was still wrapped in plastic. The date on the shipping label was from last month.

"I thought you said no one was watching this exit," Jackson said to their captor.

"I smuggled in that drysuit for you," Yung Bo said. "There wasn't one in your size."

As if Jackson was supposed to thank him. "Do you know the last time these tanks were inspected?"

"Inspected?" Yung Bo asked.

Inwardly, Jackson groaned. All scuba equipment required maintenance. He turned on a couple of the propulsion vehicles. The displays said the batteries were half-full. "Did you charge the propulsion vehicles when you dropped off my drysuit?"

Yung Bo's grin slipped. "You Americans are all the same. Greedy and lazy." His gun was still pointed at Jackson. "Too soft from taking too many vacations. You have everything you need. Make it work."

Did Yung Bo think that every American regularly went on scuba diving vacations? Yung Bo was damn lucky Jackson knew how to dive.

Jackson pulled out three suits. He set a dive computer, tank, regulator, and propulsion vehicle by each suit. "Once we leave this tunnel, how far underwater are we?"

"Forty feet," Yung Bo said.

Deep enough that they would have to manage the buoyancy with their drysuits to accommodate the changing pressure. "How much time do we have?"

Yung Bo checked his watch. "The rendezvous is in two hours."

Traveling ten miles underwater to get to the boat and dealing with unfamiliar currents was no novice dive. Jackson would have to get them suited up and teach them on the way.

He showed Min Gyu and Yung Bo how to get into their drysuits and put their tanks and regulators. He tried to condense weeks worth of dive training into a few minutes. "And if anything goes wrong, breathe out, go up, and loosen the valve on your drysuit."

Yung Bo was careful to keep his gun handy. Jackson knew he couldn't waste time or energy trying to wrestle the weapon away. Underwater, Jackson would have the advantage. And maybe if he was lucky, the Green Berets would restrain Yung Bo before Jackson had to do anything.

If the propulsion vehicles had enough charge to get them to the boat. If the oxygen tanks had enough good air. If the currents didn't work against them. Luck hadn't been on his side so far.

Chapter 28

Navy's stomach and bladder were glad when the plane landed at Camp Red Cloud. She needed stable ground, and a real bathroom. The soldiers had been using something called a comfort pallet near the cockpit. Nobody else, including Erin, seemed bothered by the idea of going to the bathroom with only a curtain for privacy.

The back of the plane opened, bringing fresh air and stars with it. Navy hurried to undo her seat belt. She could see a building nearby. Hopefully it would have a toilet with a door. Ozark stopped her before she could step off the plane.

"Refueling stop only," Ozark said. "Be quick, because I need to brief you about the jump."

The only bathroom she could find was labeled "Men," but all the stalls were empty so she risked it. Afterward, she splashed cold water on her face and waited for her stomach to settle. Of course, it didn't. It wasn't motion sickness. Navy was about to jump out of an airplane at thirty thousand feet into hostile territory, and she'd never even been skydiving before.

At the plane, Ozark was waiting next to a pile of gear that looked like the costume for an insect. If insects wore black and gray camouflage.

"There's the gadget girl," he said.

Navy would have smiled at the nickname under different circumstances. "Maybe you could tell me what all this gear is for?"

"Sorry, no time. We only have a few minutes before takeoff." Ozark was helping her into the jacket, pants, and mittens before she could object. "Don't worry. You don't need to know much. You'll be attached to me with a harness." Ozark replaced her shoes with heavy black boots and laced them up tight. Next was a harness that cinched snugly around her shoulders and legs. A tank was clipped to her harness. Then he pushed a helmet over her head and fitted the attached mask tightly. Her eyes were covered with some sort of protective goggles, and she was breathing through something like a scuba regulator. The air tasted different.

    He fitted his own mask and helmet. "Can you hear me?"

    The voice came from a radio near her ear. Navy nodded, then thought better. "Yes, I can hear you."

    Ozark's eyes crinkled at the edges, the only visible sign of his smile. "Good. We're now breathing pure oxygen. We will be on oxygen until we land. We need to flush the nitrogen from our bloodstreams. Do not remove your mask for any reason." He tapped on a dial he wore on his wrist and pointed to the one he had put on her wrist. "This is your altimeter. The main parachute opens automatically at a thousand feet. You'll feel a jerk, and then our descent will slow. If that doesn't happen and I'm unconscious, I need you to remember three things."

    It's just like climbing, Navy told herself. Release the fear and focus. "Three things," she repeated.

    Ozark pointed to a red handle on his harness. "First, you have to release the main parachute before deploying the reserve. This is the cutaway for the main parachute. Second, you need to stabilize yourself. Belly down, arms and legs out. Third, pull this handle to deploy the reserve."

    Navy was glad Ozark couldn't see her nervousness through the mask. "Got it."

    The commander waved at them from his seat, and Ozark pushed her gently toward the plane. "Keep that position the whole time, belly down, arms and legs out," he told her. "Follow my lead and you'll be fine. When we hit the water, don't forget to swim. We'll be getting on a fishing boat we hired. That fishing boat is our way back to land. Your boy should be arriving on a second boat."

Jackson, I'm coming. Navy sat down in the already-moving plane. The men around her were calm and alert. She tried to copy their focus and tap into their energy.

"You okay, Gadget Girl?" It was Erin's voice, coming through her radio.

So her nerves were obvious to everyone. "Why is everyone calling me Gadget Girl?"

"No names over the radio," Erin said.

It would have been nice if Ozark had mentioned that. Navy breathed and counted the minutes, half-wishing the jump would come sooner. Ten minutes. The mittens were getting too warm. Fifteen. She sweated through the layer of clothes underneath the camouflage. Then thirty.

"Two minutes to target," a voice said through her radio. "But, Commander, you should know . . ."

"Should know what?"

"I see our boat," said the pilot. "But there aren't any other boats for miles. Do you still want to jump?"

"We jump," said Kevin. "He's coming."

"Commander?" the pilot asked.

One of the beetle-like forms clenched his fist. Must be Kevin.

"We jump," the commander said. "Either way. Line up, team."

"Time to go, Gadget Girl." Ozark clipped the front of his harness to the back of hers.

The commander was first in line. He rested his hand on a large green crate, as tall as his waist. Kevin walked over to stand behind him. Then Erin, then Navy with Ozark, then the rest. The order must have been agreed on beforehand, because no one hesitated or jockeyed for position. Each flipped down what looked like binoculars mounted to their helmets. Navy reached up, found something similar on hers and pulled them over her eyes. Night vision? Infrared? Erin and Kevin, all of them, were barely visible. She held up her own arm and couldn't see it either. Somehow the clothing was masking the heat produced by their bodies. That would explain why Navy was so sweaty.

"Ten seconds to target," the pilot said. "Hatch opening in five seconds."

Ozark reached for a canvas loop attached to the wall of the plane.

Copying Ozark, Navy grabbed a canvas loop. She would follow Ozark's lead. She would be fine.

The roar of the wind hit her immediately when the hatch opened. Straps and carabiners rattled. Only the stars offered light. The ocean promised a cold landing.

"Deploying gear," said the commander. He and Kevin pushed the crate over the edge. Then the commander jumped. Then Kevin. Then Erin. Navy's turn.

"This'll be the best two minutes of your life," Ozark promised. Someone laughed at Ozark's comment as his weight carried Navy into the abyss of the night.

Navy was weightless. Her mind knew she was falling. The air that buffeted her neck, pulled at her clothes, roared in her ears told her she was falling. But she felt as if she were floating. She could see the roundness of the horizon. She could see the desolation of North Korea, a blank expanse of land compared to how China and South Korea glittered with lights on either side. Her altimeter counted down too quickly. Twenty thousand feet. Ten thousand feet. Five thousand.

Navy had been too distracted by the view to make sure Ozark was okay. Just in case. She opened her mouth to speak but remembered Erin's warning. No names over the radio. Keep the position, she reminded herself, as she turned her head to see Ozark. His eyes were open, focused on the approaching ocean. His eyes crinkled and he grabbed her hand, just for a second, to reassure her.

Below them, the cube of gear disappeared behind a blossoming canopy of fabric. Navy's free fall stopped with a hard jerk at her torso—at a thousand feet, just when Ozark had said their chute would deploy. For a second, she missed the weightless feeling. But it was time. She could see the choppy ocean briefly, before cold water swallowed her limbs. Navy's mask slipped and she tasted salt.

"Kick," Ozark said.

Navy was pulling Ozark under. She kicked and they floated at the surface, while Ozark's hands found the clips on her harness in the dark.

"You're free," Ozark said. "Follow me."

Navy swam after him without knowing where they were going, the adrenaline tempering the chill of the water. Finally, she saw a shape bobbing in the water. A raft with people on it. Ozark reached it first and hauled himself in. He went to grab the shoulders of her harness, but Navy copied his movements and pulled herself over the edge.

Small waves kneaded the bottom of the raft. Beside it, something else floated. Like a balloon made of raft material. More gear? One of the soldiers reached over the side.

"Found it," the soldier said, his voice echoing over the radio. He had removed his oxygen mask.

So had everyone else. Navy removed hers.

The soldier pulled a duffel bag into the raft and began to distribute weapons. Navy was given the small crate containing the drone.

Hadn't Ozark said something about a boat? She'd have to take off the mittens to operate the drone, and there was no protection from the weather on the raft. When she'd offered to fly it, she didn't imagine she'd be operating the controls with shivering fingers while floating on a thin layer of fabric between her and the infinity of the sea.

"I see our ride." The commander pointed over Navy's shoulder. Oars appeared from somewhere, and four of the soldiers began to row in the direction the commander had pointed. A fishing boat with no lights floated twenty yards away. Through her goggles, Navy could see the boat captain leaning on the railing.

Ozark's focus was on the possibly hostile sea around them. The machine gun in his hand followed his body as he scanned the horizon. Ozark never paused, and he never rushed.

The oars splashed and pulled; the relative safety of the boat grew closer. Soon the metal hull brushed against the raft. A ladder was lowered down. Ozark and two of the soldiers went first. For a tense few minutes, Navy couldn't hear anything but footsteps on the deck. Then Ozark reappeared and flashed a thumbs-up over the railing.

"Good to board, Commander," Ozark said over the radio.

"Gadget Girl, you're next up the ladder," the commander said.

Kevin landed on deck right after Navy, but he didn't acknowledge her. Still angry, then.

The boat smelled like it had been fishing recently. Buoys were lined up like sentries along the cargo area in back. Ropes were coiled and stacked neatly. The deck grew crowded as the raft emptied. The men didn't say anything, but it was clear Navy was in the way. She retreated to the tiny wheelhouse where no one else was. Near the steering wheel, she found a radar screen. Just as the pilot had said, there were no other boats. *Where was Jackson's boat?*

A boat would appear soon. It had to, because Jackson would be on it. Work would distract her until Jackson arrived. Navy opened the crate and pulled out the controller for the drone. Her cold fingers could barely pull out the antenna. She shoved her hands in her armpits to warm them.

Navy knew from the manual the drone contained an impact and altitude sensor. If it collided with the ground or fell too quickly, the sensors would trigger a short circuit designed to create a thermal runaway in the lithium-ion batteries. She couldn't risk triggering the auto-destruct with clumsy fingers.

Outside, the soldiers had stationed themselves around the perimeter of the boat. Except for one familiar form. Navy could tell Kevin was arguing with the boat captain by Kevin's aggressive posture, though she couldn't hear. She pushed the possibility of Jackson's boat not arriving from her mind and set her warmed fingers to the task at hand.

Carefully, Navy set the drone on its case and flicked a switch on top. A red light blinked indicating the drone had powered on. She turned the controller on. Next to the joystick, text scrolled on the screen.

Device found.

Handshake completed.

Ready for operation.

I should throw it in the fucking ocean. Saul and his cronies had been willing to leave Jackson to die in a North Korean prison. Why was she indulging them by piloting their little toy?

Through the dirty window Navy saw the captain throw up his hands and walk away from Kevin, toward her. Kevin didn't look appeased. The captain ducked to enter the wheelhouse, a bitter smile on his gaunt face. He was Chinese, if she had to guess. She wondered how many months' salary he was earning for this little adventure.

181

What was the right amount to pay someone to risk their life for a cause they had no part in?

"There are no boats for miles," the captain said to her. "Your friend is not coming."

Navy shook her head.

"But we will wait, because why not?" The captain gestured at the dark ocean and all its terrible possibilities. "Why not wait to see if the North Koreans will find us?"

Navy escaped to the windy deck, holding the drone and its controller. Kevin had taken up a position on the bow. Her goggles were useless for viewing the controller's screen. She took them off and turned on the screen backlight.

Holding one palm out to make a launch pad, Navy turned on the drone's rotors. The drone, already light, became a feather on her palm. The light on top turned off. With the rotors spinning, the flying machine resembled a dragonfly as its polished edges caught the moonlight.

Automatic stealth mode engaged, read the screen.

"Find me a secret," Navy whispered as the drone lifted off. If Jackson didn't come back, she would take her revenge through her work. Navy would disassemble Kim Jong Eun's regime one line of code at a time.

A low-resolution map appeared on the screen tracking the location of the drone. Navy steered the drone toward the target she had programmed in earlier, the military academy. The captain sulked in his wheelhouse. The soldiers scanned the dark, choppy water. The drone reported each GSM or CDMA signal it found. Because of the drone's small size, the battery would only last for forty minutes or so. Any phone conversations recorded wouldn't be available until the drone returned.

Her hope faded as the drone's battery drained. She knew, despite Kevin's protests, they couldn't wait forever.

Navy steered the drone back to the ship before the battery died.

The commander walked over, checking his watch. "We have to go in five minutes." He didn't mention Jackson.

In her mind, Navy saw the doctored photo of Jackson's abused body. If it wasn't real before, it would be real now. "I understand."

"There's a light." Erin's voice. "Five meters off the stern."

"Three people," Ozark confirmed. "In scuba gear."

Kevin turned from his post to look at Navy. He was grinning. "Told you I'd bring him home."

"Focus," the commander snapped. "We're not home yet."

Navy was focused—on running to the stern—but she ran into Ozark's arm first.

"We can't identify them until they get closer," Ozark said. "You'll stay back until I say."

"But—"

"In the wheelhouse, on the floor. Until I say," Ozark growled.

Of course. North Korean fucking mind games, as Eli had said. She heard the whir of the drone approaching and grabbed it from the air. It took all her self-control to walk away from the sounds of splashing at the back of the boat.

Navy sat on the floor of the wheelhouse, wishing they had given her a gun. The captain had a gun in a holster on his waist. She didn't entirely trust him. The worn holster shook as he pulled the anchor and started the motors.

"Prepare for boarding." Ozark's voice. Navy strained to listen over the motor and the waves. "We're sending down a ladder." This was louder. He was speaking to the men in the water. "Come slow now."

Navy stood so she could look over the captain's shoulder. Ozark's team was arranged in a ring around where the ladder had been dropped. The boat listed once, twice, three times, and three dark figures climbed over the edge into the crosshairs of the soldier's rifles. Ozark scanned the horizon and Navy ducked back into a sitting position.

"You two keep your hands up. You, hood and scuba mask off," Kevin said.

Was it Jackson?

"Now you." Kevin again.

Navy clamped her arms around her knees to keep from standing. Three people had boarded. Two weren't Jackson.

"Now you." But this time a flurry of footsteps followed. "Thank God."

Navy bolted through the door and pushed her way through the crowded soldiers. She barely recognized Jackson as the shivering form being helped out of a dry suit by Kevin and Erin. Partially healed cuts criss-crossed his arms.

"Navy?" Jackson blinked at her with disbelief.

Citrus and mint. The scent of him hit her as soon as she wrapped her arms around his chest. Even under the dank seawater, she could smell him. Tears of relief dripped from her chin onto Jackson's shirt.

"Jesus, it's good to see you." Jackson hugged her back, and she felt the weakness in his grip. "How—and why—"

"Long story," Kevin said. "I'm glad you're back. She's insufferable without you."

"I could say the same for you," Navy replied. She focused on arranging herself to support Jackson, who was having trouble standing.

Behind Kevin, two men were kneeling on deck. Guns bristled in a semicircle around the shivering figures. It looked more like Ozark's men were taking prisoners than granting asylum. Navy looked inside herself for compassion for the North Koreans but found only anger. Min Gyu hadn't been careful enough, and Jackson had nearly died because of it.

"Min Gyu's not so bad," Jackson said.

Navy's hatred must have showed on her face. "I don't care."

Jackson squeezed her shoulder. "Your vindictiveness is touching." His tone was light, but his eyes were haunted. Navy knew it was too early to ask what happened.

Ozark looked up from where the asylum seekers were being searched. "I told you to stay in the wheelhouse."

"The people we found were the people we expected," Navy said. "We're okay, right?"

"Stick to tech, Gadget Girl," Ozark said. "We're still in hostile territory. You and Jackson need to stay in the wheelhouse until we dock."

The boat rocked, pushing Jackson's weight against Navy. She braced herself to keep them both standing. "I need some help getting him there."

One of the soldiers supported Jackson's other side. "Easy does it," said the soldier. The boat was moving now, hitting more waves and creating some of its own.

The few yards to the wheelhouse took several minutes between Jackson's unsteadiness and the rocking of the boat. With the soldier's help, they settled Jackson on the narrow, short bunk in the wheelhouse. The dim light found the shadows between the goosebumps on Jackson's skin. Stray droplets of water balanced on the red lines of healing cuts. Had Yung Bo—the man fewer than ten yards away from her—held the knife? And how had Jackson made it this far from shore in his condition?

"Good to see you again, Jackson," said the soldier. "I'm Evan, the medic on Garrett's team."

"I remember you," Jackson said. "From a few weeks ago."

"Well, that's a good sign. But then you got yourself all the way out here so you can't be too badly off." Evan was pulling items from a med kit: a small flashlight, a silver emergency blanket, and some sort of packaged food. He handed the blanket and the food to Navy. "Open these."

Navy opened the emergency blanket first. It crackled as she wrapped it around Jackson's shoulders. Evan was shining the flashlight into Jackson's left eye, then the right eye. "Pupils responsive."

"I had antibiotics for the past week or so. While we were ... detained."

Evan nodded as he examined the cuts on Jackson's arms. "You're healing nicely. Considering. Navy, hand me that stethoscope. Got that food ready yet?"

Navy quit staring at Jackson and fumbled with the plastic-wrapped energy gel blocks. She recognized the squares from her own hiking adventures. They were basically electrolytes in bar form. Navy held a square out to Jackson.

Evan was listening to various places on Jackson's chest and abdomen with the stethoscope. Navy watched Evan's face carefully for any sign of bad news.

"No major internal bleeding, at least from what I can hear. Your blood pressure is a little weak, but that's understandable," Evan said. "In a few hours we'll get you to a real hospital where there are smarter people with better equipment than me. You should eat that whole bar. You need the energy to recover from that swim."

"So he'll be okay?" Navy asked.

Evan was already reassembling his med kit. He paused and smiled. "I've seen worse. Your boy will be fine."

"Thanks for the assist," Jackson said.

"I'm just glad this mission had a happy ending. We almost didn't . . ." Evan stood up. "We didn't see a second boat. The pilot thought we should turn around."

Jackson nodded. "Not how I thought we'd get here either."

"I have to go treat the prisoners now. Keep eating."

"They're treating Min Gyu as a prisoner?" Navy asked.

"Until they verify his allegiances," Evan said. "Or lack thereof."

"Don't treat him too harshly," Jackson said.

Evan shrugged. "I'm just a grunt, but I'll pass the word on."

Navy leaned against the cold metal of the wheelhouse so Jackson could lean against her. The blanket crackled as he shivered, and she pressed closer. As if she could make him well.

Fear, like a low-grade fever, competed with her relief at seeing him alive. She wasn't sure if Jackson had come home the same man she had said goodbye to eight days ago.

Chapter 29

Erin's email to Byron had no text, just the subject line: *Sunny day here*. The prearranged signal would tell Byron that Jackson was alive. The details could wait. Byron didn't even know Navy had social engineered her way on to Jackson's rescue mission.

Next stop, the base hospital. After the boat docked back in China, they had taken a short plane ride to Kadena Air Base in Japan. Everyone needed some time to recover, especially Jackson. Erin was given army fatigues so she would blend in. The uniform scratched at her skin. Erin had been in the army once. When she was younger, and more naïve.

This wasn't the first time Erin had visited a friend in the hospital, but it never seemed to get any easier. She was disappointed, but not surprised, to see Navy still in the chair by Jackson's bed. There were things Erin needed to tell Jackson without Navy around.

Erin knocked lightly on the doorjamb as she entered. She was careful to stay out of hugging range. Navy took the hint and settled down in her chair, stifling a yawn.

"Let me take a shift," Erin said. "You look like you could use some sleep."

"I've been resting," Navy said.

"Sleeping in a chair doesn't count." Jackson released Navy's hand. "Go. Get some sleep in a real bed."

"Well, if Erin's here, I guess." Navy rubbed her neck. "I'll be back in a few hours."

Erin looked away when Navy leaned down to kiss Jackson. Partially out of respect and partially because any display of affection left her feeling squeamish. The sound of a television bled through the wall of the next room.

"I suppose I should thank you," Jackson said after Navy left the room.

Erin shook her head. "For not saving you in that warehouse?"

"You and Kevin. Like a broken record." Jackson tried to sit up and grimaced in response to an injury Erin couldn't see. "Yung Bo had too many men. If we'd had two more units of Green Berets, maybe we would have had a chance."

"Still." Erin stared out the window. It really was a sunny day. "We're glad to have you back. Byron sends his regards." She knew what the next question would be.

"Byron still has the box of things I left for Navy?"

Erin nodded. Guilt wasn't something she felt very often. But Erin had made a promise to Jackson, and she hadn't kept it.

"I should be angry with you. Everyone thought I was dead. You were supposed to deliver the box to Navy."

"Yeah. Well." Even the memory of the sadness Erin had felt was uncomfortable to hold. The events had left her paralyzed. She was supposed to be above such emotional things. "We didn't know for sure."

Jackson raised an eyebrow. "You're blowing your cover. Someone might mistake you for human."

"You'll keep my secret." No need to ruin a good friendship by being sappy.

"How did Navy handle the news?"

Erin studied the slow-moving clouds out the window as she pondered her answer. Genuine romantic relationships were a mystery to her. Would knowing Navy's pain hurt him too much? Maybe lying would cause more problems. "She didn't leave your apartment for a week."

Jackson's expression made Erin regret her statement.

"Then she bullied Saul into putting together the rescue operation."

The words seemed to comfort him. "That sounds like her."

Erin had to escape the feelings crowding the room. "You're tired. You need to rest too."

"Thanks for coming by." Jackson was already turning his head to sleep.

"See you in a week or two."

Jackson's eyes opened. "Another mission? Already?"

"Some extracurricular activity." *Why did I say that?* Normally she kept her personal life to herself.

"Let me guess. The red-haired one . . . Ozark?"

Erin smiled. "Maybe."

Jackson's next words came out as a mumble as he closed his eyes. "Have fun."

"Always." Erin generally had few complaints about her life. But lately she'd been feeling the urge to strengthen the few close relationships she had. Navy, Jackson, Kevin, Byron. Maybe even teach a few things to Byron's daughter, Clara. Every woman should know some joint locks, just in case.

And now, Ozark. First dates that were also last dates were her specialty. But Ozark had invited her on his delayed R&R weekend, and she had accepted. She wasn't sure if she was going to run away after the first night or not.

Chapter 30

Navy wanted to find a place to be invisible, but not alone. As tired as she was, she knew she couldn't sleep right now. She needed to get away from the base. All the soldiers in uniform with guns at their hips reminded her too much of Jackson's capture and narrow escape. Too many times, Navy had imagined what Jackson's capture must have looked like. The overwhelming force of enemy soldiers . . .

Enough.

Commander Garrett had told her about a base entrance where you could catch a cab into Chatan. Navy could find a restaurant for a late meal. In any city this big, there would be a place popular with expats where she wouldn't attract attention. Maybe Kevin had forgiven her by now for inserting herself into the mission. Eating a late dinner with a familiar face might be nice.

She tried to follow the signs in the hallways back to where she had been assigned quarters, near Kevin and the rest of the team. But the signage had been confusing even when she was fully awake, and soon she was walking in circles.

"You a little turned around?"

The friendly drawl was familiar. Ozark.

"I was trying to get back to our quarters," Navy said. "But I have no idea where I've ended up."

Ozark smiled. "These big bases are always confusing. Unless you want to visit Yung Bo, you're headed in the wrong direction."

"Yung Bo can rot in hell." The words surprised Navy as much as they did Ozark. "Sorry, I'm just tired."

"Naw, I was thinking the same thing." Ozark cleared his throat. "I heard Jackson is recovering well. As well as can be expected anyway."

Navy wasn't sure the scars would be physical. "Yes, we should be able to travel home in a week."

"We're all glad Jackson made it back. Our missions don't always end this well."

I didn't think I'd see Jackson again. The statement was too intimate to share with Ozark. "Could you say thank you to your team for me? Especially Commander Garrett. He could have decided we should turn around without even jumping. And the medic, Evan."

"We wanted to finish the mission," Ozark said. "Never leave a soldier behind."

"Well, thank you. I should have said something before. I was too distracted on the boat."

"Too distracted by not following orders, you mean?" Ozark was smiling again.

"Not my strong suit." Navy managed a small smile. "I don't suppose you could point me toward our quarters in this maze?"

"Thataway," Ozark pointed where she had come from. "Then take the first hallway on the right."

"Thanks. I mean, thanks again."

"See you around, Gadget Girl." Ozark strode past her, whistling softly.

Navy found the hallway Ozark had pointed out. Rooms 484, 486, and 488 were hers, Erin's, and Kevin's. The closest door number to her was room 500. She kept going, passing room 492, 490—

"Your problem is that you're too goddamned impatient." Kevin's voice – from the hallway Navy had just left.

Navy retraced her steps, and saw Kevin slipping his phone in his pocket several yards ahead of her. He was heading toward Yung Bo and he was walking very fast, even for Kevin. What business could Kevin have with Yung Bo? Or maybe Kevin was going to see Min Gyu?

Kevin had been evasive about the whole Min Gyu/Yung Bo situation before Jackson's rescue. If Navy interrupted Kevin's errand, he wouldn't tell her anything.

She followed Kevin to the barracks but stopped short when she heard him greeting the guard.

"I'm here to see the prisoners."

"I need to see some ID." Something was pushed across a desk. "And you need to sign here."

"Are you sure?" Kevin asked.

Navy peeked around the corner, too curious to resist. A porn video was paused on the screen of the guard's computer. The guard at the desk was pocketing some cash. Cash Kevin had given him? Navy ducked behind the corner just as Kevin glanced in her direction.

"Thanks, man," Kevin said. "I appreciate it. You want me to bring these trays to the prisoners? You – uh – look like you're in the middle of something."

"I know what people say about you CIA sorts," the guard said. "But you seem all right."

"Thanks," Kevin said flatly.

A mouse clicked. Navy could hear a woman's moan now. And ... a fizzing sound? Navy didn't dare peek again. She heard the guard guzzling something, then a metallic clink as the can was set down.

"Do you have news from the State Department? About my offer?" Must be Yung Bo's voice. The details of Min Gyu's asylum package had been settled for weeks.

"They said they were thinking about the position you wanted," Kevin said. "They send their regards."

"Your assistance in this matter will be remembered."

Navy heard a tray being slid across a metal surface. Yung Bo's dinner tray?

"Mind unlocking Min Gyu's cell for me?" Kevin said. He must be speaking to the guard.

"Sure thing." The video paused for a few seconds. There were mouse clicks at the guard's desk, and the sound of a door swinging open.

"Thanks."

Navy risked another look around the corner.

There were only two cells, right next to each other. Min Gyu's cell was open, and Kevin was sitting on the bed. Yung Bo was gobbling up his dinner. And the guard was ... nodding off. What the hell was going on? Navy hid behind the wall again.

"Yung Bo's presence here makes your case more difficult," Kevin said. "But I think you already know that."

Metal clattered against concrete. Yung Bo's tray?

"What the—" Min Gyu's voice, not Kevin's. "What's going on? Why is Yung Bo grabbing his chest?"

"Yung Bo is having a heart attack," Kevin said. Navy had never heard Kevin sound so cold-blooded before.

"I don't understand. Why is—and what does—"

"You've said that you're seeking asylum because you want to see the North Korean government fail. I believe you. But not everyone does."

"But I didn't invite him—I told you—"

"As I said, I believe you. But not everyone does."

A low-pitched moan of pain now competed with the moans in the porn video. Must be from Yung Bo, mid-heart attack.

"What can I do?" Min Gyu asked. "Send the signal early? Before I get to the United States?" Min Gyu was referring to the signal that would destroy the network of North Korea's

194

nuclear weapons program. "What if they don't let me into the United States after I give them what they want?"

"Yung Bo is having a heart attack," Kevin said. "He is going to die regardless of what you do. However, your cell is now open and the person guarding you is asleep for the next five minutes."

"I don't understand," Min Gyu's voice was frantic now.

"You need to prove that Yung Bo is not your ally."

"You mean I should—"

If only Navy could see through walls. She didn't dare risk looking again. What was Kevin trying to do?

"You know what you need to do after I leave," Kevin said. "I was never here. The guard won't remember me."

Navy heard the door swing open again. Kevin, headed her way. A long, straight hallway led away from the cell block. Even if she ran, she wouldn't reach the end before he rounded the corner. So she waited. And Kevin appeared, as she had expected, a second later.

"What are you—" Kevin looked up and down the hallway. "We need to get farther away from here."

"Before what?" she demanded quietly.

"Just follow me. For the second time today, apparently," Kevin said.

Navy followed Kevin's orders but only because she wanted to hear his explanation. He pulled her along until they were nearly running. When they reached the intersection with the main hallway, they heard a gunshot from the direction of the cell block. Footsteps ran toward them. A group of soldiers, including Ozark.

"What did you do?" she hissed. She wondered why she was keeping her voice low to protect Kevin.

"Stay back," Ozark yelled as he ran past them.

Kevin didn't listen and neither did Navy. She ran down the hallway behind Kevin. A circle of soldiers was pointing their guns at Min Gyu, who was standing in front of Yung Bo's cell. A gun was at Min Gyu's feet. A circle of red was blooming beneath Yung Bo's body. The proof Kevin had asked for.

The guard stirred, perhaps woken by the gunshot. Navy saw the realization of his predicament dawn on him in three jerks of the guard's head. His gun was missing from his holster. One prisoner had shot another on his watch. And every one of the soldiers currently guarding Min Gyu could also see that he'd fallen asleep watching porn during his shift.

Min Gyu had tears streaming down his face. "I'm sorry, I'm sorry." But his eyes were unfocused. He didn't seem to be apologizing to them. "I'm sorry I couldn't shoot them all."

"Kick the gun over to me," Ozark growled.

"Do what he says," Kevin said. "You won't get hurt, I promise."

"Fuckin' hell," Ozark said as he ziptied Min Gyu's hands. "What are we supposed to do with him now?"

"Put him back in his cell and send him a thank-you card." Kevin gestured at Yung Bo's body. "No one wanted this piece of shit in the first place."

"Didn't I tell you two to stay back there?" Ozark said, shaking his head. "You both suck at following orders."

"You're right," Kevin said. "We should go."

"We?" Navy asked. At the moment, she didn't want to be associated with Kevin. Navy hadn't figured out exactly how Kevin did it, but clearly he was responsible for Min Gyu killing Yung Bo.

"Yes, *we*," Kevin said. Then quieter, just to her. "Do you really want to talk here?"

Navy wondered why she trusted him enough to keep walking next to him. "I guess not."

Chapter 31

The bar was quiet and dark, Navy's favorite kind. Kevin had chosen it.

The bartender set two canned beers down on the scarred wooden counter. A pizza topped with various kinds of sea creatures arrived soon after. The curled tentacles turned Navy's stomach. She studied the glass bottles lined up on the shelves behind the bar instead. Navy hadn't spoken to Kevin on the walk to the base entrance or the taxi ride here.

But Navy had come. She wanted to know what Kevin had to say.

"How much of what I told Min Gyu did you hear?" Kevin asked.

Navy tapped her fingers against the cold metal of her beer. "So you know what you can lie about?"

"So I know how much I need to explain."

Navy had expected a firm rebuke about state secrets, not an invitation. "And I should trust you're going to be honest with me."

"Believe it or not, Navy, I respect you."

Navy didn't entirely believe him. But there was something else in Kevin's demeanor besides professional courtesy. "You want to tell someone."

Kevin's smile was bitter. "Civilians think there's some black magic to how we keep secrets. There's not. Ninety-nine percent of the world doesn't pay enough attention to notice what we do." It was rare for Kevin to be so indirect.

Navy sipped her beer and waited.

"I respect you *and* there's no point in lying to you. You know too much."

"You told Min Gyu he was under suspicion because of Yung Bo," Navy said. "You said he had to prove his loyalties."

Kevin nodded and took a square of pizza. "Which is true. Min Gyu is in a much better position now."

"And the guard was asleep because . . ." Navy remembered the fizzing sound, but without the snap of a can opening. "You drugged his can of pop."

Kevin nodded again. "Yep."

"And Yung Bo's heart attack . . . that's why you offered to bring the meals to the prisoners. So you could poison Yung Bo."

"You're doing very well so far," Kevin said. "Continue."

Navy glared at him. "You knocked out the guard so Min Gyu could take the guard's weapon."

"True, but incomplete. Min Gyu needed a plausible weapon, and the guard couldn't be a witness, and the guard needed to be blamed."

Navy didn't know if she should start with her questions or her moral objections. "You're okay with an innocent man being blamed?"

Kevin snorted. "Innocent? Hardly. He's part of a racist offshoot of Odinism."

"The pagan religion that worships Thor?"

"I watched a bunch of the YouTube videos he subscribed to," Kevin said. "Pretty vile, hardcore stuff."

Navy shook her head. "I'm confused. The guard was a target too?"

"A target of opportunity," Kevin said. "I needed a fall guy. I wanted to pick someone who deserved it. The Odinist stuff will all come out at his court martial."

"Because you'll make sure of it."

Kevin raised his beer. "Exactly. Don't want people trying too hard to defend him."

198

"And people will believe that he just . . . fell asleep watching porn on his shift," Navy said.

"They're testing him for drugs as we speak. He makes regular trips to get cocaine in town, where multiple witnesses saw him last night. He was there getting high instead of getting his beauty sleep. That's why he was so tired today."

"Which you will make sure also comes out at his court martial."

"As is my patriotic duty," Kevin said.

Navy wished she'd asked for water instead of beer. "I don't understand. All of this effort just to . . . what? Punish Yung Bo?"

"A nice fringe benefit, I'll admit. But no." Kevin took a long drink of his beer. "Saul never found a country willing to take Yung Bo. We made a deal. Unofficially."

"You mean—"

"I promised Saul that Yung Bo would die before we reached United States soil in exchange for the mission to rescue Jackson."

"And the effects on Min Gyu? The trauma of being manipulated into killing someone? That doesn't matter?"

"Unavoidable, I'm afraid. I needed the killing to look natural."

Navy gripped her beer so hard she heard the can crinkle. "It's wrong. It's inhumane. Jackson would never—"

Kevin's hand slammed down on the bar. "You weren't supposed to be here. Why do you think I was so upset when you showed up at the hangar? You weren't supposed to know. I'm the one who took this risk."

The realization came to Navy slowly. "You don't want Jackson to know."

"Jackson can't know. He would never forgive himself."

"So I'm supposed to keep this a secret from him?" Navy knew Kevin was right. If Jackson knew the price of his freedom, the guilt would eat him alive.

"You weren't supposed to—"

"Be here," Navy said. "Got that part." If only she had left that hallway a minute earlier, she never would have overheard Kevin on the phone. Kevin waved the bartender over and ordered a cup of sake. The bartender poured it and disappeared into the shadows at the other end of the counter.

"I'm sorry you're involved," Kevin said.

"But you're not sorry you did it."

"Nope."

Navy shook her head. "I could turn you in."

Kevin tore off another square of pizza. "You won't."

"How do you know?" Navy snapped.

"Then Jackson would know how Yung Bo died. Plus, you're too loyal."

Navy wished Kevin weren't right. Again. "You're an asshole."

Kevin set his food down and wiped his fingers on a napkin. "I know I'm not a good person." His blue eyes, like shattered glass, studied her. "I have . . . instincts . . . I'm not proud of. I know how to get into people's heads and manipulate them. I chose this job, this career, because I get to indulge those instincts for a good cause."

The stool creaked as Navy shifted away from him.

"You can hate me for it if you want. Sometimes I hate myself. But you need to believe me. This was the only way I could get Jackson home. And Yung Bo? He was a pimple on the ass of humanity. The world doesn't need him."

"You can't just know—"

"I can." Kevin's voice was tight with strangled emotion. "Yung Bo didn't have to torture Jackson, but he did. You want to know what he did to earn his rank in the regime? Yung Bo ran the worst prison camp in the country. And that's a hard title to earn in North Korea. He was a sociopath who took advantage of an authoritarian regime to indulge his worst instincts."

"How is that so different from you?"

"I protect good people. You, Jackson, the rest of my agents. It's my job to protect them from spineless bureaucrats like Saul. Would you rather have left Jackson to languish in some prison camp?"

"That's not fair. You traumatized Min Gyu. You executed a man without trial. We have a judicial system. We have prisons—"

"You think I have the power to order life imprisonment? Saul and his keepers forced me into this position, Navy. They didn't want to be responsible for finding a place to keep Yung Bo. So I had a choice. Kill a bad man to protect a good one or leave a good man to die."

"And now it's my burden too." Navy already had too many secrets to keep. Two years ago the army veteran turned rogue assassin sent to kill her had been buried with full military honors. A year ago she had watched her contact, Andrei, get beaten to death for trying to protect his nephew from sexual abuse. Andrei's Interpol file still labeled him a criminal.

"How are you so sure your little operation is going to stay a secret?" Navy asked.

"You're worried about your reputation."

"I'm worried about Jackson. There's no point in me keeping this from him if he's going to find out because you messed up."

"Now you're thinking about the important things."

As if Navy were his coconspirator. "Just tell me."

"There are only two living witnesses. You and Min Gyu. He won't say anything. If Min Gyu admits killing Yung Bo wasn't his idea, people might think Min Gyu sympathizes with Yung Bo. I wasn't lying to Min Gyu. He's in a much better position now."

"And the cameras in that part of the base?"

"Do you really think the guard would have been watching porn and racist YouTube videos on his shift if the cameras were working? They haven't been working for months. The worst this base typically sees is some private who gets arrested for starting a drunken brawl."

"So Jackson gets to come home, Min Gyu gets a life in the US, and Yung Bo dies in a way that looks like it's not our fault." Navy swallowed over the lump in her throat. "It's still not right."

"It's right enough."

"I don't know how to do this," Navy said.

"Do what?"

"Keep these secrets and stay sane. Jackson and I just got to a good place. That wasn't easy. You know me. You know him."

The bartender held up the bottle of sake, but Kevin covered his glass. Kevin said something in Japanese and pushed a few bills across the counter. When the bartender left, Kevin spoke. "Remember your code."

"The virus I wrote?"

Kevin smiled. "I forgot who I was talking to. I mean a code of honor. Every officer who survives in this business has one."

"You think what you did was honorable."

"I protect my own. That's honorable. Jackson's mine, you're mine. I protect my agents and I protect my mission."

"A code of honor shouldn't be whatever's convenient."

Kevin raised an eyebrow. "Mine isn't. You remember when you and Jackson met? He asked me for help rescuing you and I told him to forget it. That you would never make it and he should stop fighting for a lost cause. He would have stopped talking to me if he'd had the option."

"And I was just beginning to think you weren't an asshole."

"Jackson is my agent. Protecting you put him in serious danger. We had a mission to accomplish and you were a distraction. It wasn't personal."

"I don't like your code," Navy said.

"Make your own then. Everyone does." Kevin had finished the entire pizza during their conversation.

Navy didn't have her own code to challenge Kevin's. "I'm glad Jackson was rescued, but I won't ever thank you for it."

"Good. I didn't rescue him for you."

Navy slid off the stool and walked out the door. She needed air. The streets of Okinawa were a dense urban and neon jungle. Bright signs and electronic billboards advertising anime characters dominated the sides of every tall building. Every few blocks she veered to avoid someone passed out on the concrete.

Happy, bubbling, drunk party goers jostled her on the crowded sidewalk. Navy slipped into another bar, very much like the first. She ordered water and a plate of noodles from a picture on the menu. Navy needed to talk to someone with a less twisted perspective on the world. Two a.m. in Japan would make it about lunchtime in Des Moines.

Sara answered on the first ring. "Hey, stranger."

"Sorry, I know I haven't called in a while." Navy couldn't think of what to say next. As the silence stretched, two more people entered the bar and settled next to her at the counter. Their conversation was sloppy, boisterous, and unintelligible.

"Where are you?" Sara asked. "What language is that?"

Navy shouldn't have called. This was a bad idea. "I . . . I can't say."

"Oh."

Was Sara angry? Navy couldn't tell.

"Are you okay?" Sara asked finally.

"I'm at a bar." Navy dodged the question. "Near the hospital." A military base hospital was probably not what Sara was picturing. And Navy was several miles away. But the description wasn't too far from the truth.

"Well, you're clearly not in Iowa with your parents," Sara said. "Is Jackson hurt?"

Navy fought the tears threatening to spill down her cheeks. Of course Sara would figure it out. Isn't that what Navy wanted? Isn't that why Navy had called her? "He was . . . is . . . hurt. But they said he'll be okay."

"I'd ask what happened, but you probably can't tell me."

"You wouldn't want to hear the whole story anyway," Navy said. *You might think less of me.*

"When do you two get to come back from . . . from wherever you are?"

"A week. And then Jackson will need some time to recover in DC."

"I'm so sorry, Navy. It sounds serious. I'm glad he made it."

"I am, too." What a ridiculous statement. *Why am I not making any sense?* "I had to do something. I mean, I didn't do it. I learned about it after it was already done. But someone did something and . . ."

"Breathe," Sara reminded Navy. "Someone did something and what?"

"I don't think it was right. But it meant Jackson could come home."

"Oh, sweetheart." Sara's sympathy made Navy nearly cry again.

"I can't tell anyone. I can't tell Jackson. I don't want him to feel guilty."

"But if you don't say anything—" Sara started.

"I'm guilty too."

"How not right was this something?" Sara asked. "On a scale of lied-about-eating-the-last-piece-of-cake to homicidal-killing-spree?"

"The people who were seriously hurt deserved it." How traumatized was Min Gyu from being manipulated into murder? Could an execution ever be considered justice? "Mostly."

Neither of them said anything for a long minute. The conversation near Navy exploded into laughter that was like sandpaper in her ears.

"Do you ever feel like you're just practicing?" Navy asked Sara. "I thought I did the right thing exposing CRYSTAL, but some people still think I'm a traitor. Last year, I went to—" Navy was thinking about the Hackerville op, but she couldn't share any details with Sara. "I canceled on you to go help a friend and I tried so hard but I didn't do everything right and people got hurt." Navy hadn't managed to save Andrei. Anna had ended up with a concussion. Had Navy called for backup sooner, things might have gone differently.

"Everyone has regrets," Sara said. "What if I'd been ready for kids five years ago? Then maybe we wouldn't be having so much trouble conceiving. What if I'd talked to my dad about his health sooner? Maybe he wouldn't have had a heart attack. There's no point in getting stuck on what-ifs."

Navy's thoughts kept tumbling, despite Sara's advice. "But what if I keep the secret from Jackson and he finds out years later and resents me for it? What if I don't keep the secret and he resents me for telling him?"

"Navy, stop," Sara said firmly. "We're all human. We're all just practicing."

Navy stabbed at the now-cold noodles with her chopsticks. "I don't think I'm going to tell Jackson why he got to come home."

"Okay," Sara said.

"What would you do?" Navy asked.

"Your story was kind of light on details," Sara said.

Navy definitely heard a touch of anger in Sara's voice. "You're upset."

"I—" Sara huffed. "I'm trying here. I can't tell you what I would do if you can't tell me what's going on."

"That's fair." The drunks near Navy stumbled out the door. Navy felt her friendship with Sara straining in the silence left behind. "I'm sorry I called. I should have just . . . I don't know."

"I'm glad you called," Sara said. "And your new life . . . these secrets . . . I'll get used to it. That's how relationships work. That's how friendship works. Our lives change, we adjust."

Navy watched the last ice cube in her glass turn as it melted. "You make it sound simple."

"Oh, it's not. But if you want my advice on what to tell Jackson, that's my answer."

"I don't understand," Navy said dully. She would have been frustrated, if she'd had any emotional energy left.

"Whatever you decide, however Jackson feels about what he knows or doesn't know, Jackson loves you. You'll talk it out. Your relationship will adjust."

"You are a better friend than I deserve," Navy said.

"I don't know about that. You've saved my life—twice now."

Navy supposed it was true. Once, she had rescued Sara after a climbing accident. But the second time. "You're forgetting about the part where it was my fault we were kidnapped."

"You've got to get over that," Sara said. But Navy could hear a smile in Sara's voice. "That wasn't your fault. This isn't your fault. Make the best decision you can. Then let the guilt go."

Navy knew Sara was right. Navy also knew Sara's advice wouldn't make her feel any better tonight. "Maybe I can start on that tomorrow."

"Call me when you land in DC," Sara said. "Let me know how Jackson is."

Navy promised and hung up. Was Sara right? Would Jackson eventually understand? Despite all the moral dilemmas she'd navigated since she met Jackson, despite all the skills she thought she had learned, she always seemed to end up in the same place. Alone with her secrets and her guilt and wondering if she was doing the right thing.

Chapter 32

Navy calculated the time difference between North Korea and DC. It was late in the afternoon at her office building, the time when people reached for coffee to make it through the last few meetings of the day. In North Korea, offices were just opening. Everyone in Min Gyu's old division would be sitting down to their keyboards.

Navy Trent was sitting in the same conference room where she had typed her messages to Min Gyu. One of those messages led Jackson into a torture chamber. Peter, the man who had accused her of being a traitor, sat across from her. Jackson sat next to her. He was still weak from his ordeals, but he had been unwilling to miss the moment. Navy would have been perfectly happy staying at home.

Kevin arrived and looked around the room. "Saul's not here yet?"

"Picking up Min Gyu's resettlement packet, I think," Jackson said.

Navy didn't like how weak Jackson's voice sounded. Any sort of exertion was still painful for him. Even after a week at the base hospital in Okinawa and a night's rest at their apartment in DC.

"How's recovery going?" Kevin asked. "Are you listening to the doctor and taking it easy?"

"Navy's making sure I am." Jackson smiled ruefully. "Despite my protests."

"Well, keep up the good work," Kevin said to Navy.

"Sure," Navy said flatly. She couldn't summon a more polite response. She wasn't sure she considered Kevin a friend anymore.

"Guess I'll find a seat," Kevin said, reading her expression. Thankfully, Kevin took a spot on the other end of the table.

On Navy's left side, Min Gyu sat in front of the laptop the CIA had given him. She had helped configure it so Min Gyu's activity wouldn't be tied to the CIA's network. Min Gyu's login to Twitter went through a few proxies and then Tor.

Uri and Eli eagerly watched the projection of Min Gyu's screen.

Navy thought of her friendship with Kevin, wrecked. Jackson's life, nearly lost. Navy's own integrity, sacrificed. All for this moment.

"When will Saul be here?" Uri asked. "What's taking so long?"

Min Gyu's Twitter account had only posted a few tweets over the past 3 years, all innocuous. His handle and bio claimed he was a South Korean woman named In Sook. He had followed a handful of other Twitter handles, but nobody who posted anything about politics. He had played his hand well. Keeping the account quiet, but not inactive, made it less suspicious.

Saul strode into the room carrying a thick manila envelope. He dropped it on the table in front of Min Gyu. "Here's everything you need for a new life. Birth certificate, passport, state ID, and the information on your apartment and bank account."

Min Gyu stared at the envelope with a blank expression then removed each document, one by one. He opened his new passport to the page with his face. "Thank you." He carefully replaced the documents in the envelope. Like a pianist, he put his hands on the keyboard and looked at the laptop screen. "Everything is ready."

Saul flicked his wrist with impatience. "Then what are we waiting for?"

Navy would be happy never to see Saul again.

Min Gyu's message pushed the blinking cursor across the screen.

"Fun trip to the zoo! #whitetiger"

After Min Gyu posted the message, he refreshed the screen. His Twitter account now had one new post. "The virus I wrote is watching for the #whitetiger hashtag on this account," Min Gyu said. "In a few minutes, the parent nodes will pick up the command and distribute it to all the children nodes."

"Excellent," Saul said. "We'll have people watching your apartment until we can verify—"

"There's no need." Min Gyu hadn't stopped typing. A new tab was open in the browser. Several squares of videos showed up in tiles across the page. Offices with people typing, laboratories full of men in lab coats, and storage rooms with boxes of records lining the shelves.

Saul's mouth opened and closed a few times before he managed to speak. "You put in cameras?"

"I didn't need to put them in. State Security did," Min Gyu said. "I just copied the footage to my server. You will, of course, be given copies."

In the storage room, smoke drifted at the edges of the camera angle. Then flames. A man rushed to the door, tried to turn the handle, but it didn't open. "And firebombs?" Saul asked.

"All of the archives are equipped with self-destruct mechanisms. They can lock from the inside to trap intruders." Min Gyu spoke with eerie calm. "I only triggered what was already there. The records you see are old weapon designs, some of them nuclear."

Navy remembered Min Gyu's original message, when he said he would "burn down the furniture factory." Navy hadn't known he meant literally.

In the offices, people looked at their screens with exasperation. The universal look of someone whose computer had just stopped working. In the labs, scientists stared at their equipment. The displays were suddenly blinking red, the universal sign of malfunction. The man locked in the burning records room was no longer visible behind clouds of thick smoke.

Saul was grinning. "This . . . is amazing."

Navy looked at Jackson. He was focused on the projected images, each a vignette of suffering or confusion. This Jackson was unfamiliar to her. She had seen Jackson happy on the rare occasions when they were relaxed. Upset when he saw people getting hurt. Angry when he felt helpless. But never this grim satisfaction. When a man was being burned to death in front of him. Navy wondered if Jackson thought his own suffering was justified.

Min Gyu was watching the bottom corner of the screen. This office looked similar to all the others, but this man had an office to himself. While most of the workers looked angry or confused, this man was frozen by whatever was on his monitor.

"Who is that?" Navy asked.

"My uncle, Sung Yong." Min Gyu answered without looking away.

Navy tried to remember the details in Min Gyu's first letter. "The one who killed your father."

"And my mother."

"How will the North Korean government know to blame him?" asked Saul.

"Every screen is displaying a letter right now," Min Gyu said. "A letter signed by my uncle. The letter says he forced me to write the code that destroyed the weapons program because he no longer believes the Kim family members are the true leaders of North Korea. He will be arrested. I will be assumed dead."

Men in uniforms entered Sung Yong's office. Sung Yong's paralysis broke. Even without audio, Navy could see the man was pleading and yelling. Sung Yong's pleas had no effect on the guards who pulled him out from behind his desk. One guard kicked him to the ground. The other ground his heel into Sung Yong's ear.

A third guard searched his desk and found a handful of thumb drives. He shook them near Sung Yong's face.

"Those are his South Korean TV shows," Min Gyu explained. "He forced me to download them for him. The government will say he was corrupted by foreign media."

"Why would he keep so many?" Navy heard herself asking as the terrifying silent movie continued. Now two guards were searching the desk. Sung Yong had been tied to his chair and blood was dripping down his face. Another man arrived. His uniform had more bars and the guards immediately stopped to listen to his orders. An officer.

"I named the files after famous propaganda films about the Dear Leader." An unnerving lightness came into Min Gyu's voice. "I lied and told my uncle I had made it so the files would only play on his computer, so he could keep them for as long as he wanted. He thought no one would ever know."

The officer pulled out a black baton and hit Sung Yong in the ribs. Sung Yong's mouth opened in a silent scream. How much of Navy's sympathy did he deserve? Sung Yong had willingly and gleefully supported a murderous regime. He had killed Min Gyu's father in cold blood and sentenced Min Gyu's mother to a slow, terrible death.

Still, the quivering pile of flesh slumped in the office chair was too pathetic to hate. "They'll torture him," Navy said. *No human being deserves that.*

"My uncle is only caught in this trap because he is guilty. My code wouldn't have caught an innocent man. Like the code you wrote to catch your president and his lies." Min Gyu looked away from the screen and skewered Navy with his expression: calm, calculating, and satisfied. "You and I, we aren't so different."

I never tried to get anyone tortured. But before Navy could protest, Min Gyu had turned back to the scene playing out thousands of miles away.

"Days from now," Min Gyu continued, "when they're interrogating him, they will tell him the final command came from a Twitter account under the name of In Sook. That is the name he gave my mother when he put her in a prison camp. Sung Yong will know it was me."

Navy followed the logic of Min Gyu's punishment to the end. "But Sung Yong won't be able to say anything. Because if he admits he put your mother in a prison camp as In Sook, Sung Yong would have to admit he knew your father was a traitor to the regime."

"As long as they don't think it's us," Saul said. "Min Gyu, despite your uh ... presentation here, we will need to verify these events. Your case officer can take you home. We'll be watching the apartment."

"If you don't mind, I'd like to stay a bit longer." Min Gyu had closed all the video feeds but the one from his uncle's office. The officer's baton swung again, this time at Sung Yong's throat. Sung Yong coughed in spasms. When the officer faced the camera again, a fine spray of blood covered his uniform jacket. Navy felt all the times she had seen people beaten. All the times the blows had been directed at her. Navy remembered her own rage and shivered at its cold-blooded reflection in Min Gyu.

Navy dropped Jackson's hand and stood up. "I have to go." She escaped into the hallway, down the elevator, out the front door. She took gulpfuls of the cool fall air to push away the weight pressing on her chest. Old memories, old violence crowded her thoughts. Recent violence kept her pulse stuttering. She had to keep moving.

Ten minutes later Navy found herself in front of the same diner Kevin had brought her to weeks ago. As if part of her still trusted Kevin. Navy rubbed her arms. It was too cold to be outside with just a T-shirt and she had left her coat behind in her rush to leave. Through the diner's windows, she saw Daisy putting on fresh coffee. *What the hell. Might as well go in and warm up.*

Navy chose a booth. "A cup of coffee and a slice of pie," Navy said when Daisy came over.

"Cherry or peach?" Daisy asked.

The simple decision was too much for Navy's tangled thoughts. "I—uh."

"Peach it is," Daisy said. "Should I make that three?"

Navy followed Daisy's nod toward the front door. Kevin was holding the door open for Jackson, who was moving slowly. "Yeah, sure," Navy said.

Jackson sat next to Navy and squeezed her shoulder. "Took us a bit to get to my car. I grabbed your coat for you."

Kevin hovered near the edge of the table, as if asking for permission. Humility? From Kevin? A ploy for sympathy? Navy couldn't detect any deceit in his posture, only fatigue.

"You might as well sit," Navy told Kevin.

The slanting light of early evening warmed Navy through the windows of the diner. She rested her head on Jackson's shoulder and looked past Kevin. Navy didn't know what to say to Kevin. Or even to Jackson. She was worried about how quiet Jackson had been since he was released from the hospital in Okinawa. Jackson had always told Navy that talking about what happened was how you process trauma.

But Jackson wouldn't say a word about what happened to him.

Navy wasn't sure what to think about herself either. Was she weak for being the only person to walk out of the room? Or should she be grateful her humanity was still intact?

She was glad for the interruption when Daisy brought three generous slices of pie and three coffees, with honey for Kevin.

Kevin stirred the honey into his coffee. In her peripheral vision, Navy saw the silver spoon winking in the light.

"Navy, I—" Kevin's unfinished sentence wilted in the air between them.

Let him squirm. Maybe Kevin hadn't intended for Navy to be involved in keeping a secret from Jackson, but now she was. Between Jackson's stonewalling and Kevin's secret, Navy could feel her relationship with Jackson changing in ways she didn't like.

"Is one of you going to tell me what's going on?" Jackson asked.

Navy took a bite of pie.

"Probably better for Navy to explain," Kevin said.

Jackson shook his head. "God, both of you are stubborn."

Make your decision, Navy told herself. *Tell Jackson about Yung Bo's assassination or keep the secret forever.* Was Jackson who she thought he was? Jackson hadn't been disgusted by Min Gyu's reaction to watching a man get burned alive. Would Jackson agree with what Kevin had done? If Jackson were okay with it, would Navy be okay with knowing that side of Jackson?

"I wasn't supposed to be on your rescue mission," Navy said. "I talked my way onto the plane and Kevin was against it."

Kevin's chin dipped slightly to acknowledge her half-truth. "She's leaving out a few details. She risked a felony to find out where the mission was leaving from, then snuck onto a military base and lied to the mission commander about being familiar with a drone so she could justify her presence."

Jackson laughed. "Nice work."

Navy should steer the conversation toward safer territory. "What happens to Min Gyu now?"

"I'm not sure what you mean," Jackson said. "You heard Saul. He has a new apartment and a lifetime salary."

Navy sipped her coffee, trying to find the right words to explain her concerns. "He can just move wherever he wants?"

"Eventually. I expect the department will always keep tabs on him. But he's not a prisoner." Jackson squeezed her hand. "Is there something you're worried about?"

"I was there right after Min Gyu shot Yung Bo," Navy said.

Kevin tensed.

"Min Gyu said *I'm sorry I couldn't shoot them all*," Navy continued. "He was apologizing to somebody who wasn't even there."

"His parents, I imagine," Jackson said. "Or maybe the American asset Min Gyu turned in after his parents were killed and his uncle had taken him in."

Navy dropped her fork. "Min Gyu turned in one of our sources? And you're okay with this?"

Jackson frowned. "It's complicated."

"Sounds pretty simple to me." Navy couldn't believe how calmly Jackson was discussing Min Gyu's betrayal.

"It is simple," Kevin said. "Min Gyu was fifteen years old when his parents died. And his uncle, the only person in the world left to protect him, was telling Min Gyu everything his parents had taught him was a lie."

"I don't think he's a bad person," Jackson said. "He was just put in a bad position."

Navy shook her head. "I wish I could believe that."

"After I was . . . detained, Yung Bo kept us locked up together in a room in a mansion," Jackson said. "Min Gyu told me a lot of things. He has a lot of guilt to work through. But that's partially why we give defectors case officers. To watch for mental stability issues."

"I still get the feeling we're going to hear about someone torturing pets near Min Gyu's new apartment a few months from now," Navy said. "And I brought him here."

"You and me and Saul and Jackson and some agency directors and a few senators and a team of Green Berets," Kevin said. "Accepting Min Gyu's defection was never decision."

"You did a good thing, Navy," Jackson said. "I know it doesn't feel like it. But watch the headlines. You'll see."

Navy rested her head on Jackson's shoulder again and watched the cars moving down the highway. Jackson pulled her closer. "You'll learn," he said softly. "You'll learn how to live with the secrets."

Kevin cleared his throat. "I think I'll head out." He pushed a set of keys across the table to Navy. "Don't let him drive yet."

"Thanks." One way or another, Navy always ended up thanking Kevin.

"You—we—made the world a slightly better place," Jackson said after Kevin left. "We had a successful mission."

"With everything that happened? You call that a success?"

"No non-combatants were harmed and we achieved our objective," Jackson said. "Yeah, I call that a success."

So that was Jackson's code. "Min Gyu was motivated by revenge, not justice."

"Thousands of families in South Korea are safer now because of what we did. Think of all the families in North Korea that will find it easier to escape as the government's power wanes. Because of what we did."

"I nearly got you killed."

"No." Jackson's arm tightened around her shoulders. "Ozark's team may have rescued me but you're the reason I made it home."

And Kevin's secret deal. "Not completely home," Navy said. "Not yet." Still leaning on his shoulder, Navy felt Jackson shake his head.

"What do you mean?" Jackson asked.

"You won't talk about what happened. Between when you were captured and when you and Min Gyu were kept at the mansion." Navy was afraid to look up to see if she had pushed too far, too soon.

"I just need some time."

"I know. And you'll have it." Navy pushed herself up. She had to say this directly to his face. "But you will come home to me. Talk to a therapist or me or one of your friends. Someone."

"That sounds an awful lot like advice I gave you once. Or twice."

Navy tapped him on the nose. "Then perhaps you should follow it."

"You win." Jackson smiled. "I promise. Now if you're not going to finish that pie . . ."

"It's all yours." Navy watched Jackson eat with gusto, glad his appetite was returning. "I think I understand better now. Why it was so hard for you when I agreed to go to Hackerville. You felt responsible for me going."

"Protecting someone you love is a strong instinct."

Yung Bo's body, splayed in a puddle of his own blood, appeared in Navy's mind. And Min Gyu, standing over him. *I couldn't kill them all.* Kevin was many things, but he was right more often than not. If carrying the secret of Yung Bo's execution was the price of having Jackson home with her again, she would pay it. "Yes, it is."

Epilogue

Jackson was surprised by the knock on the apartment door. Through the peephole, he saw Byron holding a shoebox. The box Jackson had told Erin to give to Navy if Jackson had died. When Jackson opened the door, Byron walked in without being invited.

"Please, come in," Jackson said as he watched Byron go into the kitchen.

"I figured I should return this to you." Byron set the box on the counter and helped himself to a beer from the fridge.

"And make yourself at home," Jackson said.

Byron smiled and plopped himself into a dining chair. "Why thank you, I think I will."

Jackson had been looking forward to some time alone in the apartment. While he appreciated Navy's concern for him, her constant focus on his mental state was starting to feel claustrophobic.

"My wife kicked me out of the house because of her book club meeting," Byron said. "And Clara's out with Navy doing a spa day. So I thought I'd come visit you."

Navy had mentioned she was going to spend the day with Clara, Byron's daughter. "Navy? At a spa?" Normally, the only time Navy let strangers touch her was in sparring matches at the gym.

Byron laughed. "Yeah, Clara really had to talk her into it. But a little relaxation would be good for Navy."

"Definitely," Jackson said. "Clara will be a junior when school starts this fall, right?"

"She and her friends are renting this house off campus," Byron said. "I remember what my friends and I did the first time we had our own space."

"Threw a big wild party?"

Byron nodded. "I know there are some mistakes I have to let her make. But it's a residential neighborhood. I could introduce myself to some of the neighbors, give them my number just in case . . ."

The term helicopter parenting could have been invented for Byron. Sometimes Jackson wondered if his friend was overcompensating for being gone so much of Clara's early life. Jackson let his skeptical expression speak for itself.

"You're right, that's too much," Byron said. "Anyway, let's talk about how you haven't been answering my texts for days. Clara told me it's called ghosting."

Inwardly, Jackson groaned. Of course that's why Byron was really here. "You and Navy have been talking, haven't you?"

"She's worried about you."

"I told her I just need some time." Jackson tried to count the days that had blurred together since he was rescued.

"It's been a month," Byron said. "Navy says you haven't been to any of the appointments Kevin made for you with that therapist."

"I . . ." Jackson couldn't give Byron any of the bullshit excuses Jackson had been telling himself for canceling the appointments. Byron was too good a friend. Jackson also couldn't lie and say he was planning to go to the next appointment. "I know I promised Navy I would talk to someone," Jackson said. "And I will. Eventually."

Byron didn't look convinced.

"I counsel people. I am a trained psychologist." Jackson paced the kitchen. "I know how to get people through trauma." It wasn't that going to a therapist seemed like defeat, exactly. It was that Jackson knew what the therapist would say. The same things Jackson would say.

"So you think you can be your own psychologist. You think you can talk yourself through this."

Jackson crossed his arms and leaned against the counter. "Well, it sounds ridiculous when you say it."

"There's a reason surgeons don't operate on themselves."

Jackson's mind jumped to the tools surgeons use. Like the tools brought out on a cart in the room where he was tortured. The flash of anger and helplessness and pain was debilitating. Jackson closed his eyes, felt the counter take more of his weight. Jackson could hear his own heartbeat.

"Jackson? What did I say?"

Jackson blinked his eyes open. Byron was standing in front of him.

"You should sit down for a minute," Byron said.

Jackson let Byron lead him to a chair. *Breathe slowly*, Jackson told himself. He let his head rest in his hands. *Steady now.* His pulse slowed. He felt Byron's hand on his shoulder.

"You're not okay," Byron said. "Before you went to North Korea, you'd seen a lot of death and misery. We both have . . ." Byron shook his head as if to clear his own thoughts. "Everything you experienced while you were captured is on top of that."

Jackson thought of the soldiers in his unit he'd watched die in Bosnia. They had—he had—been helpless to stop the massacre of a group of civilians inside the church. He remembered how many bombed-out houses he'd seen in Afghanistan. Children's shoes littering the yard. Helpless again. As hard as he'd tried to get weapons into the right hands – and out of the wrong ones – it was never enough. And barely a month ago. Tied to a chair. Helpless while— no. He couldn't face it. Not yet.

"Trauma is cumulative," Jackson heard himself say. A line he'd read in a textbook but never applied to himself before.

"Exactly. You think everything you've been through means you can get through this without help. But you don't have to. And you shouldn't try."

Jackson took a shaky breath. "My next appointment is on Monday. If it's up to me, I won't go. Will you drive me?"

"Glad to."

"Thank you." Jackson's head felt clearer now. He straightened and looked around the apartment. Lately, even familiar places felt odd to him. Not foreign, exactly. Just . . . different. Returning to this apartment after each operation, especially now that he shared it with Navy, had always grounded him. Recharged him. But since he had returned this last time, he felt as if he were drifting. As if any moment everything he loved could be separated from him.

"Navy will be relieved," Byron said.

Navy. Jackson felt a rush of guilt. "Navy's upset with me because I won't talk with her about what happened."

"I don't think that's why she's been upset," Byron said. "At least, that's not what she's been telling me."

"But why can't I?" Jackson asked. "I don't understand why it's so hard to share this with her."

"You really don't know?" Byron shook his head, amused. "I'm no psychologist and even I know the answer to this one."

Jackson tried not to glare at his friend.

"You want to be Navy's protector. You always have. You don't want her to think you're weak."

The remark stung. Jackson swallowed his pride to consider the idea. "I guess I thought I was more enlightened than that."

"Believe me, I wish I were more enlightened." Byron rolled the bottom of his beer on the table. "Every once in a while I get these bouts of insomnia. Can't sleep for two or three nights in a row. Nancy would try to talk with me... and I just couldn't. Not with *my own wife*. I was gone for half of Clara's childhood. Nancy had to deal with everything all on her own. And I still feel like I should be playing man of the house."

"You two are the closest to happily ever after of all the couples I know. At least, I thought you were."

Byron shrugged. "I've been lucky in a lot of ways. Nancy and I might have our problems but we've been happy together, more or less. Didn't seem right for me to be complaining to you."

"I thought I was having trouble talking to Navy because we've only been together a couple years," Jackson said. "And it wasn't exactly normal, the way we met."

Byron laughed. "Not exactly. Anyway, I promised Nancy I would go to therapy. And I did. And now the insomnia's better. And the discussions are easier. Sometimes."

"You, in therapy?" Jackson asked.

"Don't look so shocked," Byron said.

"You'd never mentioned your insomnia was that bad before. Or that you and Nancy ever had issues."

"I quit fieldwork so I could be home more. And I don't regret it. Mostly. But we hadn't really discussed what it was like all the time I was gone. How hard it was for her to be alone in a new city without any family around." Byron paused. "Nearly fifteen years, and we never talked about it because I hadn't worked through my own shit."

"I think this operation was especially hard for Navy," Jackson said. "She blames herself for me having to go at all."

"You're missing the point. Stop focusing on Navy. She'll be fine, if you are."

"You're enjoying this a little too much." Jackson was used to being the one giving advice.

Byron puffed out his chest a bit. "I am, actually."

"I've always told Navy that accepting help doesn't mean you're weak," Jackson said.

"You've always been bad at taking your own advice." Byron took another swig of his beer. "You ever wonder if we work for the CIA because we have some sort of hero complex?"

Jackson smiled for the first time in days. "I prefer to think of it as an extreme tendency to exhibit altruistic behavior." His stomach growled. Even feeling hungry seemed novel. For the past few weeks, he had eaten for sustenance, not pleasure. "Should we order pizza?"

"Pepperoni for me," Byron said.

Jackson ordered a large pizza then got a beer from the fridge. He realized he hadn't hung out with a friend in a long time. Jackson raised his beer in a toast. "To dumbass heroes."

"Cheers." Byron clinked his bottle against Jackson's. "Hey. I have to ask."

"You want to know what's in the box I left for Navy," Jackson said.

"Something heavy and metallic. Erin and I were trying to guess. A collection of safe deposit keys for every bank in the city? A small bit of radioactive material shielded with lead?"

Jackson shook his head and smiled. "I'm surprised you didn't have it X-rayed."

"Give me a little credit," Byron said. "I have *some* self-restraint."

Jackson looked at the innocent-seeming box on the counter. "I collected all the stripes and bars off my uniform from when I was in the army. And my medals from that NATO mission in Bosnia." Jackson thought of that disastrous last mission. Until a couple months ago, it had been the worst thing he'd gone through. "I wanted Navy to give them to my family. My dad was disappointed when I left the army. I guess I just wanted to remind him of how proud he was when I joined." The medals Jackson had been given seemed more shameful than honorable. He'd been the only one to survive. "I couldn't tell him I was going to work for the CIA when I left. My family still thinks I work in imports for some store. My dad half-jokes about it sometimes. Says I quit being a hero to work in retail. He was in the army most of his life."

"My dad and uncle were both in the army. I still have a cousin in the coast guard," Byron said. "He's always bragging about his latest rescue and joking about how working as a librarian must be *so exciting*."

"You could have chosen a more exciting cover story than librarian at a law firm," Jackson said. "Rodeo clown maybe?"

"Good to see your sense of humor is back." Byron finished his beer just as someone knocked on the door.

"Pizza's here," Jackson said. "Let's save the discussion of our inherited hero complexes for the next time you want to play therapist."

Byron smiled. "Maybe my next challenge should be getting Erin to talk about her childhood."

"Bring a bulletproof vest," Jackson suggested.

***

Navy dropped Clara off at home then drove to the office. She went to a floor she didn't normally visit, where the North Korean analysts worked. She heard Uri and Eli before she could see them. They were nicknamed the dueling twins for a reason.

"This officer is talking about a military exercise with China," Uri said emphatically.

"No, they're talking about a North Korean labor camp in Russia," Eli insisted.

Navy knocked lightly on the doorjamb.

"Navy!" Uri turned to see her. "These conversations the drone recorded are gold."

"Oh, good." Navy was still angry the drone had been a condition on Jackson's rescue mission. But her curiosity had won out. "Thanks for letting me sit in."

Uri and Eli could have easily refused her request to see the translations of what the drone had recorded. Access to intelligence was generally limited to what you needed to know for a specific assignment.

"What did you get?" Navy asked.

"Names and places, mostly," Eli said. "We can fill in some gaps in the military hierarchy. And they've mentioned a couple places where they're printing counterfeit money."

"They're into counterfeiting too?" Navy had learned a lot about the various international crimes of North Korea over the past few weeks. But this was new.

"Oh, yes," Eli said. "Do you remember the Seán Garland extradition case? There was an offshoot of the IRA that helped North Korea launder fake American currency all over the world. Some of the best made forgeries ever done."

Just when Navy thought the story of North Korea couldn't get any weirder. "If only we could hear what they're saying now," Navy said. "With everything Min Gyu did, so much has changed." How long could the dictatorship in North Korea last without a functioning nuclear weapons program?

"Working on this operation was a once in a lifetime opportunity," Uri said. "Don't you feel lucky?"

Clearly Uri and Eli did.

Navy didn't. She imagined everything she'd done in the past couple months stacked on a scale - good deeds on one side, bad on the other. Which way would the scale tip and according to whom?

Navy knew the answer, as unsatisfying as it was. How the world judged her was less important than following her conscience. *The only way forward is through*, Navy thought.

Acknowledgments

There comes a point in editing a novel where the finish line seems unreachable. I imagine it must be like when marathon runners hit the "wall." There are just too many edits, too many missing scenes, too many imperfections for the project to ever be completed.

This novel in particular has felt like a slog. COVID-19 hit during the middle of the final rewrite. Relative to many in the United States, I've been lucky. But the mental weight of watching my country's initial botched reaction to a pandemic and the fevered conspiracy theories that followed is still a heavy one.

I could write a whole novel about how it feels to live during this transformation.[1] Half the country (myself included) is waking up to exactly how much work the United States has to do before we are all considered equal. The other half is doubling down on a misguided, toxic nostalgia. We used to have a stronger middle class and invest more in public infrastructure and social programs, that's true. But there's a lot in American history, even recent history, to be ashamed of.[2]

I pushed through the wall to finish this novel because writing is what I'm driven to do. But I never would have made it without help. Once again, my editor Dara Syrkin has encouraged me to murder my darlings. And comments from beta reviewers like Christopher Gales, Bridget Kromhout, and Ry4an Brase are always helpful in saving me from myself.[3]

To the very short list of people who have been waiting for the next Navy Trent novel, I'm sorry it took so long. Knowing you're waiting means something, and I hope the book doesn't disappoint.

A human practicing,
Megan

1. In fact, the next Navy Trent novel is largely about the miasma of racism, sexism, and conspiracy theories swirling around in the United States. And watching friends and family get seduced by them.
2. Rigid social norms and hierarchies have always been worse for the non-male and the non-white in America, but these hierarchies are bad for everyone in the end. As Whitman wrote, "I am large, I contain multitudes." We all deserve a chance to be our best selves, even if that's different from what's expected of us. Learn how to shoot a gun and crochet a beanie. Pump iron and study interior design. Drive a big truck and read Walt Whitman. Be a farmer who sings Broadway tunes in the shower. Just show up for your fellow humans. We're all just practicing. Which leads me to ...
3. Writing is great for revealing all your inner warts. During one of the scenes in this novel, I kept referring to the soldiers as "the men" when one of them was Erin. Writing the chapters with Irving/Kevin illuminated just how many of the preconceptions about the "dirty, inner city" still live in my head, even though I also live in the city. Whitman again, "Do I contradict myself? / Very well then I contradict myself, / (I am large, I contain multitudes.)" It's hard to take these moments of shame and instead turn them into moments of self-reflection. But I'm trying and it gets a little easier every time.

Printed in the USA
CPSIA information can be obtained
at www.ICGtesting.com
CBHW010846050924
14101CB00044B/705

9 781734 759020